She would have to tell Rory the truth about what had happened after their summer together

Except she had tried. And he hadn't cared enough about her to return her phone calls when she'd desperately needed to talk to him nearly six years ago. His silence had added an exclamation point to their argument about maintaining a long-distance relationship.

She'd lost that battle—in spades.

But she'd won something more precious.

Now the time had come when she had to face up to reality. But first she had to determine what kind of man Rory had become. There was more at stake than her own heart.

She tried to remember another time in her life when her emotions had been so volatile. Or when procrastination had seemed like a perfect solution to whatever dilemma she faced.

Soon—*very* soon—she would have to tell Rory he had a five-year-old son....

Dear Reader,

This month Harlequin American Romance delivers favorite authors and irresistible stories of heart, home and happiness that are sure to leave you smiling.

COWBOYS BY THE DOZEN, Tina Leonard's new family-connected miniseries, premieres this month with *Frisco Joe's Fiancée*, in which a single mother and her daughter give a hard-riding, heartbreaking cowboy second thoughts about bachelorhood.

Next, in *Prognosis: A Baby? Maybe*, the latest book in Jacqueline Diamond's THE BABIES OF DOCTORS CIRCLE miniseries, a playboy doctor's paternal instincts and suspicions are aroused when he sees a baby girl with the woman who had shared a night of passion with him. Was this child his? THE HARTWELL HOPE CHESTS, Rita Herron's delightful series, resumes with *Have Cowboy, Need Cupid*, in which a city girl suddenly starts dreaming about a cowboy groom after opening an heirloom hope chest. And rounding out the month is *Montana Daddy*, a reunion romance and secret baby story by Charlotte Maclay.

Enjoy this month's offerings as Harlequin American Romance continues to celebrate its yearlong twentieth anniversary.

Melissa Jeglinski
Associate Senior Editor
Harlequin American Romance

MONTANA DADDY
Charlotte Maclay

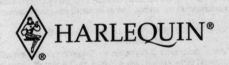

HARLEQUIN®

TORONTO • NEW YORK • LONDON
AMSTERDAM • PARIS • SYDNEY • HAMBURG
STOCKHOLM • ATHENS • TOKYO • MILAN • MADRID
PRAGUE • WARSAW • BUDAPEST • AUCKLAND

Special thanks to Karen Kay, historical romance writer extraordinaire, who has been honored by the Blackfeet nation for her efforts to encourage literacy within the Indian community. Thanks for being my friend.

ISBN 0-373-16980-9

MONTANA DADDY

ABOUT THE AUTHOR

Charlotte Maclay can't resist a happy ending. That's why she's had such fun writing more than twenty titles for Harlequin American Romance, Duets and Love & Laughter, plus several Silhouette Romance books, as well. Charlotte is particularly well-known for her volunteer efforts in her hometown of Torrance, California; her philosophy is that you should make a difference in your community. She and her husband have two married daughters and four grandchildren, whom they are occasionally allowed to baby-sit. She loves to hear from readers and can be reached at P.O. Box 505, Torrance, CA 90508.

Books by Charlotte Maclay

HARLEQUIN AMERICAN ROMANCE

Don't miss any of our special offers. Write to us at the following address for information on our newest releases.

Harlequin Reader Service
U.S.: 3010 Walden Ave., P.O. Box 1325, Buffalo, NY 14269
Canadian: P.O. Box 609, Fort Erie, Ont. L2A 5X3

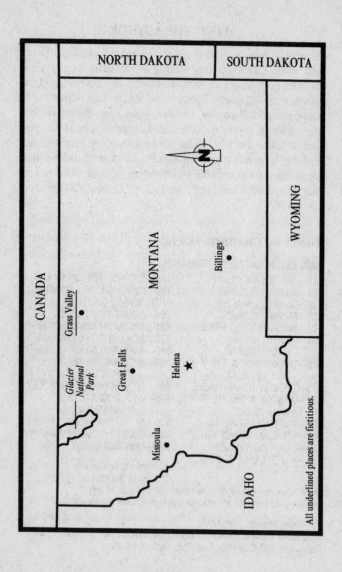

All underlined places are fictitious.

Chapter One

"I'm going to break my fool neck if somebody doesn't help me out of this truck!" The penetrating voice of Dr. Justine Beauchamp cut through the chilly afternoon quiet in Grass Valley, Montana.

Across the road from the medical clinic, Rory Swift Eagle Oakes smiled to himself, tugged his black Stetson down more firmly and ambled toward the unfamiliar SUV that had pulled up in front of the old three-story Victorian house. As a kid he'd thought the dormer windows were like eyes and the occupants were watching him.

Now he and the often cantankerous doctor were colleagues of sorts. She took care of the two-legged patients in this northern part of the state, and he handled those with four. Plus a few two-legged birds of prey who fell victim to hunters or tangled with power lines. Doc Justine, for all of her years in this part of the world, didn't have much interest in rehabilitating injured hawks and eagles. Or wolves and elks, for that matter.

For Rory, that was the best part of his job as a veterinarian.

"You think you could hurry a little?" Doc complained. "I'm tired of being a prisoner in this tin can."

"I'll be right there," came a muted reply from the SUV's driver.

A couple of days ago, the doctor had slipped on some ice and gone down hard. She'd broken her ankle, which required a trip to Great Falls for surgery. Obviously, someone had brought her back home—a friend from Washington, according to the license plates.

Rory grinned again. He could imagine what a fun two-hour trip from the hospital to Grass Valley that must have been with Doc and her sharp tongue.

"I'll get her," he called to the driver of the truck, who was exiting the vehicle on the far side. He opened the passenger door.

"About time," the doc muttered. Her leg was propped at an awkward angle, a cast on her foot up to her calf.

"Quit your complaining, Doc," he said. "You'll give Grass Valley a bad name."

"I never complain. Patients are the ones who complain."

He swallowed a grin. "Whatever you say, Doc." She wasn't a big woman, probably weighed less than a calf, so he slipped one arm beneath her thighs, the other around her back and hefted her out of the truck.

Turning, he almost collided with a younger woman who was standing there. Her features were so familiar, so unexpected, her appearance drove the breath from his lungs. She had the same clear-blue eyes he vividly remembered. The same vibrant, strawberry-blond hair.

His muscles went weak from the collision of memories, and Doc Justine nearly slipped from his arms.

She grabbed him around the neck. "Young man, you drop me and I'll have you up on charges of assault and battery on an old lady. What would your brother, our venerable sheriff, think of that?"

Rory adjusted his grip on the doctor but he didn't answer. He couldn't. Kristi Kerrigan's eyes had him ensnared like a jackrabbit in a steel trap. How many years had it been? Could it be more than five? It felt like a hundred. Or maybe it had only been yesterday. She hadn't changed a bit. If anything she was more beautiful now than she had been when she'd visited her grandma Beauchamp that long-ago summer.

The summer before he'd entered veterinary medicine school.

Kristi was the first to break eye contact, jerking her gaze away from Rory.

"I'll get the front door, Grandma."

"You do that, honey, before our resident Indian chief dumps me on my rear end."

Ignoring the doc's comment about him being a chief, Rory followed Kristi up the short walkway to the structure that served as both clinic and home for Justine. The sway of Kristi's hips in snug-fitting jeans mesmerized him, the swing of her hair at the collar of her heavy jacket tantalized.

She held the door open for him, and he brushed

past her, catching the scent of apples, fresh and simple. Still her signature scent. And the memories of that all-too-brief summer came rushing back to him again.

"Where to, Doc?" he asked, eyeing the stairway to the second floor. Display cases filled with antique medical equipment that looked more like torture devices than life-saving equipment lined the entry. The entrance to the clinic was on the left, the family living room on the right, and the bedrooms were upstairs.

"First thing, I need to use the facilities at the end of the hallway. And stop ogling my granddaughter. She's too good for you."

"Yes, ma'am." He wouldn't argue with Justine's assessment of their relative merits, but he was going to have trouble not ogling. Kristi was like the first breath of spring coming on the heels of a long, hard winter.

A winter that had lasted for more than five years.

"If you can get her into the bathroom," Kristi said, "I can take it from there."

"Young lady, I've been taking care of myself for better than seventy years. I think I can manage one more time, bad ankle or not, thank you very much."

Setting Justine on her feet—or at least on one foot—Rory backed out of the small bathroom.

"Call if you need me," Kristi said as the door swung shut.

The hallway was narrow. Barely enough room for them to stand opposite each other, Kristi hugging a pair a crutches in her arms like a favorite pillow to ward off bad dreams.

Taking off his hat, Rory fiddled with the brim, shaping the felt into a smooth, curving line.

"The doc's getting crustier every year." His tongue felt as if it was glued to the roof of his mouth, and his voice was husky with the effort to speak past the raw ache of emotion in his throat. She was so darn beautiful. He hadn't realized how much he'd missed her.

"It's part of her charm."

His lips eased into the suggestion of a smile. "It's good to see you, Kristi."

"You, too." Her gaze focused on the doorknob, not on him.

"You haven't changed a bit."

Her head snapped around, a blaze of irritation in her blue eyes. "Yes, I have. I'm almost six years older and ten pounds fatter than when you last saw me."

In a lazy perusal, he took in her appearance, noting the subtle changes—her breasts a little fuller, her hips more womanly. "On you it looks good."

Her cheeks blossomed with a rosy blush, and she huffed, looking away again. "Thanks for helping me with Grandma. You can go now."

"That sounds like you want to get rid of me."

"I do. I have to get Grandma settled, fix her something to eat. No need for you to hang around."

Her curt tone was meant to cut, and he felt a youthful stab of rejection. "Are you going to be staying long?"

"A few days. I'm not sure yet."

He tapped his hat back onto his head and, sliding his hands into his jeans' pockets, he nodded. "Give me a call if Doc needs anything."

"I'm sure we'll get along fine without you."

What the hell was the matter with her? The summer they'd met she'd been as sweet as a newborn colt, prancing and dancing, filled with excitement about the future. Together they'd experienced the first bloom of young love. At least, he had.

Then they'd moved on with their lives. Within days he'd been so overwhelmed with his medical studies that he'd barely been able to keep his head above water academically. She'd probably been in nearly the same fix with her premed courses. She sure hadn't found the time to call him.

When they'd both headed off for school, he'd been afraid a long-distance relationship wouldn't work. He'd even told her so. She'd argued they could manage it.

It hadn't taken long to discover he'd been right.

He shrugged, pretending indifference. "Maybe we'll have a chance to get together before you leave, talk about old times."

She started to speak, but before she got a word out there was a staccato knock on the front door, and it opened.

"Yoo-hoo, it's only me! Hetty Moore." The owner of the general store swooped into the house, a heavy winter jacket covering her floral-print dress, a casserole dish in her hands. "I saw the car outside and thought— My sakes, is that little Kristi all grown up?''

Kristi eased past Rory, grateful for the interruption. With his chiseled features, burnished complexion and midnight-black hair, he was simply too potent, too masculine for her comfort. And he brought back far too many memories she'd valiantly tried to suppress. Her emotions were bouncing all over the place—residual anger, a too-foolish joy at seeing him and a clawing fear that her return to Grass Valley might be a terrible mistake.

There'd been no way she could refuse her grandmother's request to help her—not the woman who had been her mentor and had once saved her life.

She'd known that in coming here she would have to face Rory sooner or later. She'd hoped for a little more time to adjust to the idea, to prepare herself for what she had to tell him. As usual, when it came to Rory Oakes, her wish hadn't been granted.

"Hello, Mrs. Moore. How are you?"

"Fit as can be. And aren't you just as pretty as ever. Isn't that so, Rory?"

He'd come up behind Kristi, close enough that she imagined she could feel the heat of his body, his raging metabolism. Her own flesh warmed at the thought, the memory of how he had once held her in his ardent embrace. In the hallway, he'd towered over her. Even now with her back turned to him, he dominated the entire room and every molecule of her awareness.

"Yes, ma'am." he said. "I was just telling her that."

With hands that trembled, Kristi set aside her grandmother's crutches and took the casserole dish from Hetty. "Thank you. I was just going to fix something for Grandma to eat. She hates hospital food."

"It's only hot dogs and macaroni but it's one of Justine's favorites. Can't think why she didn't ask a neighbor to pick her up in Great Falls instead of having you come all this way."

"Yes, well, she wanted me to—"

From the bathroom Justine shouted, "You folks gonna strand me in here forever? Somebody bring me those darn crutches."

"I'll get 'em."

Rory reached past Kristi for the crutches, and she quickly scooted out of his way. Even so, she caught the scent of his sheepskin jacket, an elemental fragrance much like the man himself. He wore his cowboy hat low on his forehead, shadowing his dark eyes and concealing his jet-black hair, creating the air of a loner.

There was another knock on the front door.

"That'll be Marlene Huhn," Hetty said. "Probably bringing some of her German potato salad for Justine to gag down. She uses too much vinegar, you know."

Involuntarily, Kristi's lips puckered. She remembered the dish from church potlucks. "I'll let her in."

On the porch, she discovered Valery Haywood had arrived along with Marlene Huhn. The two women, their faces etched from years of exposure to the Montana sun, squeezed inside together, not wanting the other one to get a head start on the latest gossip.

"I brought some ham mixed with the string beans I put up from the garden last summer," Mrs. Haywood said. "Thought Justine would enjoy some veggies."

"I brought my hot potato salad. Made it special for Justine."

"That's very thoughtful of you both." Without a free hand to take the dishes, Kristi gestured toward the kitchen. "Could you put them in the refrigerator for me?"

"Ja, we can do that. How is Justine? We all just felt awful about her falling down," Marlene said, still a trace of a German accent in her voice.

"She's a little cranky but I'm sure—"

Justine hobbled into the living room on her crutches, Rory helping her. "You'd be cranky, too, little girl, if you had to haul around twenty pounds of plaster attached to your foot." With an irritated sigh, she plopped down on the chintz-covered couch.

Kristi rolled her eyes. In her experience as a registered nurse—and more recently as a nurse practitioner—doctors made the worst possible patients. Her grandmother was no exception. The next couple of weeks, while Justine recovered from her injury and Kristi assisted with her medical practice, were going to be difficult at best.

Within minutes, more neighbors arrived until the refrigerator was crammed with casseroles and the kitchen table covered with cakes and pies. Most of the ladies stayed to visit, crowding into the small living room.

"Tell us, Kristi," Hetty said, "what have you been up to these past few years? Your grandmother never talks much about you or your mother. How's your family, dear?"

Justine snorted. "I don't gossip like some folks I know, if that's what you're getting at. I've got better things to do with my time."

Kristi's gaze slid to Rory, who was standing on the far side of the room. He'd removed his hat and was smiling at her, his dark eyes filled with amusement at the antics of the well-meaning town busybodies. Her heart lunged at the sight of him, skipping a beat, and an unwelcome ache of loneliness filled her chest.

Mentally she redefined the next two weeks from *difficult* to *impossible.* That she had agreed to come here at all was clear evidence she'd lost every ounce of good sense she'd ever possessed.

The very last thing she wanted was for Rory to be privy to a conversation about her and her family.

"Ladies, I know my grandmother appreciates your concern and all the food you've brought, but she's had a long, difficult few days since she broke her ankle. Give her some time to catch up on her rest. Then she'll be happy to visit with you, I'm sure."

Holding her breath while the neighbor ladies said their goodbyes, Kristi deliberately avoided looking at Rory, which didn't prevent her from feeling his gaze on her. Boring into her psyche. Probing her secret thoughts.

Her sense of guilt brought a flush to her face, and she knew darn well she looked as guilty as she felt, like a five-year-old who had snitched more than one cookie from the cookie jar. Which in a way, she had.

Finally, after the others had left and the room grew quiet, Rory got the hint.

"Guess I'd better be going, too." He sauntered across the room toward her.

"Yes, that would be best—for Grandma."

"Shoot, honey," Justine said, "those folks brought us enough food for an army. Might as well ask Rory to stay for supper."

Kristi blanched. "No, I don't think—"

"Thanks, anyway, Doc. I've got an injured elk in my back pen that I've got to feed. He fell through some thin river ice a couple of weeks back and got stuck." He tugged the collar of his coat up around his neck, winked at Kristi and lowered his voice. "I've never been too fond of Marlene Huhn's potato salad, anyway."

By the time the door closed behind Rory, Kristi knew she wouldn't be able to draw an easy breath until she was miles from Grass Valley and her secret was safe again.

She'd been a fool to come here at all, no matter how much her grandmother had begged on the phone from her hospital bed. The people of Grass Valley could drive a few extra miles for the next two weeks if they needed doctoring.

She shouldn't have risked returning to the town—or the man who had broken her heart. Forget her conscience had been bothering her for years for not telling him the truth. *He'd* been the one who hadn't returned her phone calls. *He* was the one who'd found someone else.

Her stomach knotted in despair.

She would be the one to suffer if she didn't confront Rory and her fears. Until she did that, she'd never be able to get on with her life, because no other man had ever come close to comparing with her memories of Rory.

THE YOUNG ELK SCRAMBLED to the far side of the chain-link enclosure, his injured foreleg making his gait awkward. He turned to glare at Rory with his huge brown eyes and pawed the ground, kicking up dirt and the remnants of the last snow storm.

"It's all right, youngster." Rory broke the skin of ice from the watering trough, then forked some hay into the feeding bin. "Another week or so, and you'll be good to go again."

It had been lucky some local snowmobilers spotted the elk trapped in river ice or the animal would have died. Rory, as the area's only veterinarian and a wild-life rehabilitator, got the call to rescue the animal. At the time, the elk hadn't been too appreciative of Rory's efforts.

He still wasn't being exactly friendly.

Which was good. Rory had no intention of making the elk a pet. Just the opposite. He intended to return the elk to the wild as soon as the youngster was able to keep up with the herd. Rory didn't want the animal to become dependent on humans for either food or comfort. Generally, elk and deer did well in confinement and returned to the wild without a problem.

He stabbed the pitchfork into the pile of hay and let it rest there. April was always a tough month this far north, almost to the Canadian border. Winter had gone on too long; the warmth of spring was weeks off yet. Summer was only a vague promise.

Only the sturdy—or obstinate—survived in this climate. He figured he was a little bit of both.

Tugging the pitchfork free, he ambled back toward the clinic and outbuildings, which were adjacent to the small clapboard house where he lived. Grass Valley wasn't a big town—a single main street boasting of a general store, a drugstore that sold more ice cream than antibiotics, a busy saloon and a garage surrounded by derelict cars—all of which Rory could see from his couple of acres of land a block away.

Beyond the little town a pine-covered hill rose above a shallow river. The slash of dirt and rock left by a landslide last summer still scarred the hillside, and if it hadn't been for Rory, his brothers and Joe Moore, the tumble of boulders would have blocked the river, flooding the town of Grass Valley. Instead they'd blown big rocks into little ones, allowing the flow of water to continue downstream. A pretty nerve-racking day, as Rory recalled.

Pausing near the walkway to his house, he glanced across the street to the medical clinic and let his thoughts slip further back in time.

When Kristi visited her grandmother nearly six years ago, Rory hadn't anything to offer her for the long term. He'd been little more than a kid himself, about to enter veterinary medicine school and not all that confident he would be able to finish the rigorous course of study. His past included years in foster care, a few adolescent brushes with the law and finally adoption by Oliver Oakes, who had owned the Double O Ranch outside of town.

He'd had no guaranteed future at all.

Now he had a veterinary practice and a home that belonged to him and the Bank of Montana—in unequal shares. Plus, he was steadily wearing down the balance due on his student loans.

But from the way Kristi had avoided his gaze and her less-than-eager greeting, he doubted she'd be interested to learn he was making a success of himself.

He shoved his hands into his pockets and concentrated on the sounds of Mother Earth—the wind moving through the bare branches of the elm tree in his front yard, the crackling of dry grass as a rabbit dashed unseen through the vacant land nearby, the flight of a hawk's wings through the air.

Jimmy Deer Running, the chief of the Blackfeet tribe on the nearby reservation, had told Rory not to resent the past but to learn from it. That wasn't always an easy thing to do. Hell, most of the time he wasn't even sure what lesson he was supposed to be learning.

Like why Kristi had never called or written to him after their summer together.

Why the hell didn't you call her?

In retrospect, that seemed like a big mistake.

Maybe that explained her standoffish reception today. Maybe she was mad at him. Or maybe she was having the proverbial morning-after regrets some five-plus years later. He supposed he couldn't blame her in either case.

Women were so darn hard to understand.

Glancing up at the darkening sky, he wondered if the predicted storm front was still moving their way from Canada. Spring weather could be the pits. Just when you were ready to get rid of winter, bam! another wicked storm would come through, and you'd be ready to move to Arizona.

Of course, as soon as the storm passed and the wildflowers bloomed, you'd remember Montana was God's country.

Until the next winter.

Instead of going into his house to eat supper alone and watch reruns on TV, he decided to check in with his brother Eric. He could see the lights were still on in the sheriff's office on Main Street.

Maybe he could talk ol' White Eyes into having a beer with him at the Grass Valley Saloon, which featured "good eats" according to the banner that had hung in the window for as long as Rory could remember.

Tomorrow he'd start getting reacquainted with Kristi. She wouldn't be around long. He intended to work as quickly as possible.

Smiling to himself, he sauntered toward Main Street.

Not many men get a second chance.

As she was trying to rearrange too many casserole dishes into too small a refrigerator, Kristi happened to glance out the kitchen window.

Rory.

Her breath caught at the sight of his easy stride as he headed toward the center of town. Long and lanky, strolling along as though he had no cares in the world.

Meanwhile, her thoughts were a jumble.

Soon—*very* soon—she'd have to tell Rory the truth about what happened after their summer together.

Except, she had tried, more than once. And he hadn't cared enough about her to return her phone calls when she'd desperately needed to talk to him nearly six years ago. His silence had added an exclamation point to their argument about maintaining a long-distance relationship.

She'd lost that battle—in spades.

But she'd won something more precious.

Bless her grandmother's heart. Kristi had sworn Justine to secrecy when the doctor had discovered her secret. Good as her word, Justine had kept her confidence all these years.

Now the time had come—had *nearly* come, Kristi mentally corrected—when she had to face up to reality. But first she had to determine what kind of man Rory had become. There was more at stake than her own heart.

Her eyes fluttered closed momentarily, and she tried to remember another time in her life when her emotions had been so volatile. Or when procrastination had seemed like a perfect solution to whatever dilemma she faced.

Soon—*very* soon—she would have to tell Rory he had a five-year-old son, Adam, the true love of her life.

Chapter Two

The Grass Valley sheriff's office boasted two cells, which mostly gathered dust, a potbellied wood stove capable of giving off enough heat for a volcano, and an assortment of chairs used mostly by the locals when they came in to visit with Eric.

A police radio was located on a console to one side of the room, always set to both police and emergency frequencies. The doctor's office was hooked up to the same system. A useful tool in an area where ranches were far apart, cell phones didn't always work and emergencies were as unpredictable as spring weather.

At the moment, the sheriff was sitting behind his desk talking on an ordinary phone. From his grim expression, Rory guessed Eric wasn't having a social conversation.

Giving his brother a nod, Rory shed his jacket and hat and hung them on a peg near the door. While he waited for Eric to get off the phone, he idly thumbed through the latest stack of Wanted flyers on the corner of his brother's desk. Fortunately he didn't recognize anyone.

"What's up?" Rory asked when his brother finished his phone call.

The chair squeaked as Eric leaned back. Unlike Rory, who wore his hair collar length, Eric trimmed his in a short, almost military style. It seemed to fit with the neat cut of his khaki uniform.

"Storm's coming our way," Eric said. "A bad one, according to the state Disaster Management Agency. They want me to implement our emergency plan."

Rory cocked his brows. "Have we got one of those?"

"Sure we do. I gather together all the movers and shakers in our fair community and alert them there's a blizzard coming."

"They probably know that already from watching TV," Rory pointed out.

"Possibly. Nonetheless, it's not official till I tell 'em."

"If you don't tell them, does that mean the blizzard won't show up?"

Eric's brows pulled together in mock concentration. "I don't think that's how it works. I'll check with Disaster Management next time they call."

Chuckling, Rory sat on the corner of the desk. In a small town like Grass Valley, layers of bureaucracy weren't much use, and his brother knew that. "So when's the meeting?"

"Tonight at seven." Eric opened the top drawer of his desk and pulled out a slender telephone directory. "I'll get the preacher to open up the church—we'll establish that as a shelter, if we need one. Then I'll give folks a call, tell 'em we'll be meeting there."

"You need me to come?"

"You bet. Not only are you going to have to treat any animals that get themselves into trouble, you're going to have to fill in for Doc Justine since she's still in Great Falls."

"Nope. The doc's back. And her granddaughter, too."

Eric lifted his attention from the telephone directory and shot a questioning look in Rory's direction. "Kristi?"

Self-consciously, Rory shoved away from the desk and crossed the room to the stove. The mere mention of Kristi's name made him sweat, and the heat of the stove was no antidote, so he edged toward the cooler air near the window. "Kristi picked the doc up at the hospital this afternoon and brought her back here."

"You saw her? Kristi, I mean."

Rory tried for a shrug of indifference but felt as if it came off too stiff. He was still stunned by seeing Kristi again and the wash of memories that had swept over him. "Yeah. I helped her get the doc into the house. She's got a cast on her leg and using crutches."

"So how'd Kristi look? Glad to see you, I bet."

Hardly. "We didn't talk much. She was anxious to get the doc settled in."

"So is she married? Got kids or anything? Man, I remember you were so hot for her, I thought you'd burn up—"

Rory whirled. "We didn't get to talk much, okay? Now, don't you have a blizzard to prepare for or something, instead of sticking your nose in where it doesn't belong?"

Giving Rory a knowing grin, Eric waved off his comment. "I get the picture. You're still hot for her."

"Leave it alone, White Eyes."

"Whatever you say, Bird Brain."

The exchange of their youthful nicknames recalled the years they'd grown up together at the Double O Ranch. Eric, as the fairest of the three adopted brothers, had been dubbed White Eyes. Rory was tagged with Bird Brain after his Indian naming ceremony; his brothers took the position that Swift Eagle was too classy for him. Walker, the eldest of the three, picked up the name of Sharp Shooter—Sharpy for short—after he'd accidentally shot himself in the leg while showing off with their father's rifle.

How any of them had survived adolescence still amazed Rory, and was due entirely to the patience and wisdom of the late Oliver Oakes, their adoptive father.

"Tell you what," Eric said. "I'll get things started here by calling the preacher, and you go talk to the doc. See what kind of supplies she has on hand, what procedures she'll be able to handle—"

"You can call the doc yourself. She can talk just fine. Nonstop, if complaining counts."

"It'll be faster if you talk to her. At least you'll understand her medical jargon better than I can."

That might be true, but Rory didn't have any urge

to see Kristi again so soon. Actually he did, but she'd made it pretty clear she wasn't eager for him to drop by. It'd be better to give her a little time. Let her relax, get used to the idea of him living right across the street. Then maybe he could figure out why she'd been so torque-jawed with him.

All business now, Eric picked up the phone and started punching in numbers. "Come to think of it, ask Kristi to come to the meeting tonight. She can be the go-between for Doc."

Rory considered arguing with his brother but he knew he'd lose. Eric could be darn determined when he chose to be, a trait that had nearly cost him a leg riding a rodeo bull.

Kristi had been determined, too. Set on having a career. In no hurry to marry and have a family.

In that regard they'd been in agreement.

More than once Rory had wondered if that had been a mistake.

"KRISTI! You're going to kill yourself!"

Doc Justine's scream and a loud thumping noise propelled Rory through the door to the clinic and into the front hallway.

He came to an abrupt halt and tipped his hat to the back of his head.

Kristi was sitting on her rump at the bottom of the stairway, a double-bed mattress curved on the stairs behind her. Her face was red, and she looked out of breath.

"Are you okay?" he asked.

"I'm fine. I was just showing Grandma the latest

rage in Spokane—the wild mattress ride. Tons of fun.''

Rory's lips twitched but he didn't dare let loose with the laugh that threatened. "I'm sure it will sweep the nation in no time." He reached down to help her up.

She managed without him. "You could have knocked, you know."

"Yeah, but I would have missed the next winner of World's Funniest Videos."

She eyed him with a hostility that wasn't entirely convincing, given the twinkle of humor he spotted in the depth of her baby blues. "Things got a little out of hand," she admitted.

"I can see that. What were you trying to do?"

"Besides kill herself?" Justine asked from the couch in the living room.

Kristi ignored her grandmother. "Grandma can't get up the stairs on her crutches. Her arms aren't strong enough."

"I told her I could manage," the doc groused. "She wouldn't believe me."

"So I wanted to set up her bed downstairs," Kristi continued. "Things didn't go quite as I had expected."

"You could have called me. I would have helped."

"That's what I said, too," Justine said, loud enough to rattle the door on it hinges. "But she's the most stubborn girl I've ever seen. Don't know where she gets it. Not from my side of the family, you can be sure of that."

Both Kristi and Rory shifted their attention to Justine and burst out laughing.

Rory regained his composure first but he hoped Kristi never would. She had the most wonderful laugh, light and airy like a songbird in flight yet filled with warmth and caring. He could go on listening forever.

"Tell you what," he said when Kristi's laughter subsided. "I'll help you bring down and set up whatever you need."

"No need for all the fussing," Justine insisted. "I can sleep on one of the examining tables until I can get around on my own."

"You'd probably fall off, Grandma, and break something else. Besides, I'll be examining patients on those tables."

Rory started. "You're going to examine patients?"

She glanced at him, then looked away. "I'm a nurse practitioner. The whole idea of me coming here during Grandma's recovery is so she can see patients, as needed. I'll be doing exams under her supervision."

Surprise and disappointment combined to make Rory blurt out, "You didn't go to med school?" He'd been so darn sure, so confident she'd go the limit. Nothing would stand in the way of her goal of becoming a pediatrician.

She bristled, her spine straightening until she was her full five feet five inches tall, the top of her head barely coming to his chin. "Some of us have responsibilities, Mr. Oakes. We can't always do what we want to do."

Justine snorted. "He's not 'mister.' He's got a piece of paper that says he's a doctor, though I sure as hell wouldn't want him to treat me for a case of rabies."

Kristi looked up at him, a mixture of sadness and admiration in her eyes. "Grandma mentioned a couple of years ago that you'd graduated," she whispered.

"By the skin of my teeth and pretty well near the bottom of my class, but yeah, I got my license."

A sheen of tears suddenly blurred Kristi's vision, and she had to look away. She was so proud of Rory and so angry that he had achieved what he'd set out to accomplish when she hadn't quite made the grade.

Her own fault, she reminded herself. A premed student should have been more careful about birth control. A dumb mistake, one that had cost her a medical school education and her dream of becoming a doctor. She'd opted for fewer years of training, switching her goal to nursing so she could be home more with her baby.

In all fairness, that same mistake had been her greatest blessing and biggest joy—her son. She'd give her life to protect Adam from harm. Which is why she'd left him home with her mother while she helped Doc Justine. She had no idea how Rory would react to learning at this late date that he had a son, and she didn't intend to risk having Adam hurt.

Nor was she eager to race into the uncertain world of a custody battle across state lines. She had a friend in Spokane whose divorce left her flying her two young children to Arizona three times a year to be with their father. Her girlfriend spent the entire time the children were gone worrying about them.

Turning to resume wrestling with the mattress, Kristi ignored a twinge of conscience. Despite the fact Rory hadn't returned her phone calls, and had apparently found another woman at college almost before Kristi had gotten back home, he did have a right to know about his son.

She *would* tell him. But not right now.

Squeezing partway up the stairs, Rory grabbed the opposite side of the mattress. "Where do you want the bed set up?"

"The living room," Kristi said.

"No way," Justine insisted, her hearing in far better condition than her ankle. "Everybody who comes in will gawk at me like I'm some sort of a freak. Plant me in the second exam room. We can only handle one patient at a time, not that I ever have more than that, anyway."

Kristi risked a glance in Rory's direction and was snared by the intensity of his dark-eyed gaze. She swallowed hard.

"It's her medical practice," she said. "Her house."

"Darn tooting it is," Justine shouted, "so there's no sense to argue."

He hefted the mattress easily. "Lead the way, Nurse Kerrigan." He took a step, then halted. "Are you still Kerrigan? Or did you get—"

"She's still available, young man, if that's what you're asking. Not that she'd tumble for somebody who pokes needles in cows for a living."

Heat raced to Kristi's cheeks. "Grandma, if you don't behave yourself, I'm getting in my car and going back to Spokane right now."

"No, you won't. You're too much of a pushover to leave your old granny on her own. You wouldn't be able to sleep nights if you did."

God help her, Justine was right about that. There was little Kristi could refuse her grandmother. She owed Grandma her life...and her son's. It had been Justine's quick work the night of Adam's birth that had saved him.

Sighing, Kristi pointed to the clinic door. "If you can carry the mattress in there, I'll bring the box springs."

"Should I get my video camera to record your encore stair descent?"

She was tempted to stick out her tongue at him, but his boyish grin was far too endearing. She remembered how frugal he'd been with his smiles when they'd first met, making each one precious to her and a major accomplishment. With every smile he'd sent in her direction, she'd floated on a sensual cloud of happiness for hours.

"Why don't you let me handle moving the bed while you give the doc something to knock her out?" Rory suggested mildly.

"I heard that! You can't get rid of me that easily. And don't think I don't know what you two young people are up to. I watch TV, you know."

Kristi stifled a laugh. *Impossible* was quickly becoming an understatement.

"I'll get the bedding," she said, and headed up the stairs.

With Rory's help it didn't take long to set up the bed in the exam room. Even so Kristi fumbled with the sheets and blankets, intensely aware of a subtle undercurrent of intimacy in their task. Which was ridiculous. They were making a bed but it wasn't *their* bed.

As a nurse she'd made up thousands of beds.

But never with a lean-hipped, broad-shouldered, hunky man of Native American descent, a man who had been the subject of her fantasies for more hours than she cared to admit. So much so that she hadn't been able to develop a relationship with any other man. No one had compared to her memories of Rory.

Maybe hospitals would have more success recruiting nurses if they came equipped with men who looked like Rory. When she got back home, she'd drop a note in the suggestion box. Probably get a bonus for the idea, she thought, fighting off a bout of hysteria.

How in the name of heaven was she going to survive two weeks in Grass Valley with Rory showing up on the doorstep every few hours? She was going to have to start an epidemic of mad cow disease to keep him occupied and out of her hair.

Getting over him—putting the past behind her— was what she needed to do if she was ever going to move on with her life. That meant she had to face him and somehow find the courage to tell him the truth.

Not an easy ambition to achieve.

She watched as he smoothed the blanket over the sheets. He did have the nicest hands, long tapered fingers and a broad palm. Gentle hands, she remembered. Hands capable of arousing her to heights she'd only imagined.

"Eric's calling an emergency meeting tonight at seven. He'd like you to come."

…hands that stroked and caressed…

Her head snapped up. "What?"

"Eric. My brother. He's the sheriff now. There's a big storm coming, and he's organizing us to do what we'd do anyway without being told. Which is to help out anybody who gets into trouble because of the weather."

She blinked, trying to replace the sensual images that had filled her head with something more prosaic like the weather. "Why does he want me there?"

"In Doc Justine's absence, you're the designated emergency medical coordinator, or something like that. The disaster-planning people are real good about creating important-sounding titles." He picked up a pillow, fluffed it and plopped it on the bed. "He could probably make you director of medical services, if you'd like that better."

"No, *coordinator* is fine. Is the storm really going to be that bad?"

"They could be playing Chicken Little, but the satellite photos on the weather channel look pretty intense. I'd say don't count on spring for a few weeks yet."

She understood about planning for a disaster. You hoped it didn't happen but you needed to be prepared. Leaving Justine alone for an hour or so to attend the meeting wouldn't be a problem. Grandma could manage on her own for that long.

"Where's the meeting?" she asked.

"At the church. I can come by and get you."

Definitely not a taxi service she needed or wanted. Keeping the widest possible distance between herself and Rory was a far better choice, at least until she got her bearings and her courage built up. "I remember where the church is. I'll be there at seven."

"Great." He stood back from the bed as far as the tiny examination room would allow. "Anything else you need from me?"

How about a couple of hours of great sex? "No, I think I've got everything under control for the moment." Everything except her suddenly overactive libido. Damn!

He picked up his jacket from the top of the autoclave where he'd draped it and settled his hat on his head. "Okay, I'll see you later then."

She smiled weakly. That's exactly what she was afraid of.

THE TEMPERATURE had dropped and snow had begun to fall by the time Rory walked the couple of blocks to the church. Already the big flakes had covered the bare spots in his yard and turned Main Street slick with the white stuff. If this kept up, as predicted, they'd have a foot of snow by morning. Maybe more. Add some wind and let it snow for a few days, and the disaster-planning folks would have something to do with their time.

Helluva spring thaw.

When he reached the church, he glanced around to see if he could spot Kristi walking or her SUV in the parking lot. No such luck.

The rec hall adjacent to the church felt hot compared to the outdoors, and Rory shrugged out of his jacket. Eric was up front talking with Reverend McDuffy, a gray-haired preacher who managed to mix practical wisdom with his biblical messages.

Joe Moore, who owned the general store, was chatting with Harold Hudson, the local pharmacist. Pauline Bennett, who'd inherited her husband's plumbing business stood off to the side. She had access to a backhoe that could be needed in a snow emergency and knew how to fix frozen pipes.

"Hey, Pauline," Rory said.

"Hey, yourself. Heard Kristi Kerrigan is back in town."

"Yep." If the phone lines went down in Grass Valley, the entire town would dry up with no gossip to feed on.

"She was such a sweet girl. I remember that summer when she visited her grandmother and you two were—"

"I've gotta talk with Eric. Excuse me." With little grace, he veered away from Pauline. God, had everyone in town known he and Kristi were involved? He supposed so. Being discreet probably hadn't been on his mind. Still, you'd think after all these years people would forget. Their whole affair had only lasted six weeks.

Not that he had forgotten a minute of it.

The door to the rec room opened again, bringing with it a rush of cold air and Kristi, all bundled up in a ski jacket, her vibrant hair tucked under a knit cap. Her cheeks were red from the winter air. So was the tip of her nose. Rory couldn't remember a more beautiful sight. An eye feast for a starving man.

He smiled. "Welcome to spring in Montana."

"Spokane gets snow, too."

"In April?"

"Well, not like this, I suppose."

Eric called the half-dozen people in the room together before Rory could respond. "Let's gather around, folks. I don't want any of us to be out in this weather any longer than we need to be."

They pulled some chairs together in a circle. Rory made sure he was sitting next to Kristi, their chairs nudging each other's so there could be a chance brush of their thighs, denim to denim. A graze of his forearm across hers, sweater to sweater. She wasn't married. *Available,* according to Doc Justine. What was the matter with the guys in Spokane? Why hadn't one of them snapped her up by now? Not that he wasn't grateful for a second chance.

Distracted by the sweet fragrance of Kristi's apple-scented shampoo, Rory had trouble following Eric's comments. The only emergency he felt was the strain against the fly of his jeans. It'd be damn embarrassing to pop the zipper just sitting here. He'd have to fake it, saying something about how they don't make zippers like they used to. Nobody would believe him, though. They'd know damn well he still had the hots for Kristi. He always had.

Slowly he became aware the room had gone quiet. He looked around to find everyone staring at him.

"So what do you think?" Eric prodded.

"Um, about what?"

Eric made a vague gesture with his hands suggesting he knew Rory hadn't been listening. "Are we going to have cattle getting into trouble in this storm?"

Rory straightened in his chair. "Not if the ranchers have been paying attention to the weather reports. They'll bring the cows into their home pastures." He glanced toward Pauline. "Some of them might still need your backhoe to get in to feed them but mostly I'd say they'll be okay."

Joe Moore said, "In my experience, it's folks that do something stupid in a bad storm, not dumb animals."

"Let's hope everybody has enough sense to stay off the roads," Eric commented. "I don't have any urge to start digging folks out of snowbanks."

"There're a couple of families that live hand-to-mouth," Joe said. "If the storm lasts too long they could be in trouble, and the phone lines will go down first thing."

Reverend McDuffy spoke up. "I'll get the cots out and ready in case we need to use the rec room as a shelter."

"I can use my snowmobile to transport supplies or people if they need to get to the shelter," Rory volunteered.

"Or if they're injured," Kristi added, "you can bring them to the clinic."

Harold finally spoke up. "I've got a good supply of pharmaceuticals on hand for anybody who gets sick."

"Right." Eric nodded and glanced around the room. "I'll keep that in mind. But let's hope things don't get that bad. Well, it looks like we have our ducks in a row. Unless anyone can think of something else, I think we're done here. Thanks for coming tonight."

Rory didn't want to drag out the meeting any longer than necessary, and he stood when the rest of the group did.

"Can I walk you home?" he asked Kristi.

"I drove, thanks."

"Oh, okay. You got chains?"

"Snow tires and four-wheel drive." She made for the door. "I'll be fine."

"Maybe I should drive you. It was really coming down hard before the meeting."

She nailed him with an annoyed look. "It's all of two blocks back to the clinic, and I have driven in snow before, Rory. I'll manage."

He grimaced. "Right. You'll be fine. I was just thinking how cold and wet I'm going to get walking back to my place. But that's okay. I'm used to this kind of weather."

Her blue eyes cut through him like lasers. "You're trying to make me feel sorry for you, aren't you?"

"No, not me." He fought a grin. "Well, maybe a little."

She threw up her hands in defeat. "Oh, all right. Come on. I'll drive you home."

"Want me to follow you, Kristi?" Eric asked. "The roads are a mess."

She visibly clenched her teeth. "I think I can make it."

"And you don't need any protection from my brother?"

"Not in this lifetime," she muttered, stalking toward the door.

Making a fist, Rory make a threatening gesture toward his brother. "Follow us at your own risk, White Eyes."

Eric only laughed, and Rory hustled to catch up with Kristi.

The truck had the advantage of getting them out of the wind, but it was still icy cold. The seats crackled with it, and their breath fogged the inside of the windshield. The wipers struggled to clear the snow away, leaving frozen half circles on the glass.

"So do you work at a hospital in Spokane?" he asked as Kristi let the engine warm up.

"Actually, it's a low-income clinic. We serve mostly itinerant workers. I see the patients first and handle routine problems like colds and flu or stitching up a cut. More serious injuries I refer to the doctor."

"So you're practically a doctor."

She glanced at him, then shifted into gear. The headlights bounced off the curtain of falling snow as she eased forward. "The American Medical Association doesn't see it that way."

Behind them Rory noticed the headlights of Eric's four-wheel-drive patrol cruiser snap on. There were some serious disadvantages to having brothers who tended to stick their noses into a man's business. Not that Rory wouldn't do the same, given a chance.

Leaving the parking lot, the rear end of Kristi's truck slid sideways before the tires caught hold. She handled the skid with skill and followed the tracks left by Joe Moore's vehicle when he'd preceded them out of the lot.

"How long before the plow comes by?" she asked.

"They concentrate on the Interstate. In a storm like this, it might be days before we see a county plow. Some of the locals usually get out their Jeeps with a scoop on the front to keep things moving here in town. Nobody bothers with the ranch roads." Which is why his brother Walker hadn't come into town for the emergency meeting. Too much chance of getting stuck.

"I'm glad I got Grandma home before all this mess started," Kristi said.

So was Rory. He'd hate to think of Kristi out on the highway with this much snow falling. It would be too easy to go off the road or get stranded with no one to help her.

"Why don't you pull in at your grandmother's place? It'd be easier and I can walk across the street."

"Your veterinary clinic is that close?"

"Yep. Only a couple of patients have gotten the two clinics mixed up though. I take their temperature, give 'em a rabies shot and send them home. Haven't had any complaints."

She sputtered a laugh. "That's probably because none of them survived."

Deep snow made the turn into the medical clinic drive a challenge, but Kristi made it just fine, parking near the front door. Rory admired her skill even as he wanted to linger in her company.

They both got out, and Kristi started up the steps to the porch.

"I'll come in with you. Just to make sure the doc's okay." And maybe he'd talk Kristi into making a pot of hot chocolate. It was a perfect night for cuddling in front of a fire, listening to a little music. Making out.

"I haven't been gone long. I'm sure she's fine."

Kristi opened the door, and Justine's voice carried out to the porch.

"How long has he been unconscious?"

A woman responded over the sputter of static on the emergency radio set up in the clinic. Justine stood beside the radio, a crutch under one arm and the microphone in her hand.

As Rory listened to the conversation, he realized Doc Justine had a patient in trouble—Everett Durfee, who lived with his wife, Jane, in a remote cabin miles from town.

Rory suspected this was likely to be a long night for everyone when headlights flashed across the front windows of the clinic. He knew Eric had heard the tail end of the same emergency transmission on his car radio, and he'd come to the doc's place to deal with the crisis.

When illness struck in this weather, isolation was

more than a lifestyle choice. It became a life-and-death issue. And could put more than one person at risk.

Cuddling with Kristi and a pot of hot chocolate no longer seemed a possibility.

Chapter Three

"From what Jane tells me, it sounds like Everett was shoveling snow and had a heart attack. He's unconscious, but he has a pulse and is still breathing. He staggered inside before he collapsed."

Leaning back against the radio table, Doc Justine still had one crutch propped under her arm, and she looked worried. None of her flippant, complaining airs now. She was all professional.

Rory was impressed, as he always was, with how committed to her patients and up-to-date Justine was for a small-town doctor. Given the number of medical journals he'd seen around her office, she worked at it.

"How do you think Jane is holding up?" Eric, who had followed them into the house, shrugged out of his heavy jacket and hung it on a peg near the door.

"The Durfees are both proud and hard as nails, which is why they've survived this long living like a pair of hermits. But Jane doesn't have enough arm strength to haul her husband out to their Caterpillar tractor if he's nothing but deadweight." She shoved away from the table, and Rory helped her to a nearby chair.

"I'd hate for her to try to drive that thing in this kind of weather," he said. "Even assuming she could get Everett onboard."

"I agree," Eric said.

"How far away do they live?" Kristi lifted her grandmother's leg and shoved a stool under her injured ankle.

"About twenty-five or thirty miles east as the crow flies," Rory said. "There's a dirt road that winds around for closer to sixty than thirty miles."

"Jane also said they had three feet of snow on the ground before this storm hit, another foot's fallen since."

The Durfee cabin was about as isolated as you could get, located near the headwaters of the Willow River. Not exactly a tourist destination.

Kristi looked puzzled. "If they are so remote, how do they have electricity to run the radio?"

"A gas-driven generator," Rory explain. "It's powerful enough to run the radio or a few lights but that's about all. They heat with a wood stove and use kerosene lamps."

"This is one city girl who can't imagine living that far removed from civilization," Kristi said with a dubious shake of her head.

Eric brought them back to the crisis at hand. "Would it help if we could get some medicine to him?"

"I told Jane to give him an aspirin if he regained consciousness. But that isn't going to help much."

"Sounds like he needs to be in a hospital," Kristi said. "Preferably in Great Falls. He needs an IV and ought to have resuscitation equipment on hand, electric paddles to restart his heart if he goes into cardiac arrest."

Justine snorted. "Their cabin doesn't come equipped with that kind of gear. If someone doesn't get to Everett pretty darn soon, we could lose him."

"You have portable equipment here, don't you, Grandma?"

Rory eyed Kristi, wondering what she was thinking. Getting to the Durfee cabin on a sunny, summer day wasn't easy. The current conditions would make it a serious challenge.

Leveling her granddaughter a stern look, Justine said, "Don't even think about it, child. Your mother would kill me if something happened to you."

"But he may die if he doesn't get help. Surely there's some way—"

"There isn't," Rory said. "Not for a greenhorn."

"How about a helicopter?" she persisted.

"Not in this weather. You'd need a tank or a bulldozer to get there, and then it would take hours to go that far."

Eric held up his hand. "Not so fast. A snowmobile could make it."

Kristi brightened. "There, you see?"

"You can't mean to send Kristi out there on her own." Rory was appalled his brother would even consider the possibility. "For one thing, she'd probably freeze to death before she got a mile from town. And if she made it that far, she'd probably get lost.''

"Not if you went with her as a guide.''

The room went very still. Only the low hum of the shortwave radio broke the silence. And everyone was looking at Rory.

"I'd go myself, bro,'' Eric continued, "but I've got to stay in town to organize the disaster plan. Besides, you know the area better than anyone else.''

Rory looked for an escape route. Granted, he could probably find the Durfee cabin in a blizzard, but he didn't want to put Kristi at risk. He wasn't worried about himself. He'd gone out in rougher weather than this to rescue or doctor animals. Kristi hadn't. She didn't know what she was up against. The threat of frostbite. Getting lost and disoriented in a howling storm. Freezing to death. No way would he let her go on her own.

"How 'bout I take the gear to the Durfees,'' he said. "I can do an IV as well as Kristi, and your heart monitor can't be all that different from the one I use during surgeries.''

"I told you they were proud folks, young man. I can't see Jane letting a veterinarian treat her husband no matter how bad off he is. If we're gonna do this, Kristi has to go, too.''

"I'm willing,'' Kristi said. "It's not like I haven't been on a snowmobile before. I'll be fine.''

Rory glared at her, but she wasn't going to back down. *What the hell!*

"You think Everett will last till morning?'' Rory asked.

Justine considered her answer. "His health has otherwise been good, and he's as strong as a horse. He's got a better-than-average chance to last out the night."

"That's good, because trying to make it to that cabin in the dark and in this storm would be asking for more trouble than anyone could handle. Myself included."

"I agree," Eric said.

Rory figured the fat was in the fire, so to speak. No way could he back out. "Okay, we'll take two snowmobiles, one of them pulling a sled. We can bring Everett back here, then we can figure out how to get him to Great Falls. And Jane can ride double on the second snowmobile. She'll want to come along with Everett."

Justine nodded her agreement. "That seems like a reasonable plan to me. I can trust you to take care of Kristi. And with her there, Everett could hold on till the weather clears a bit if necessary. We can be in touch by radio."

His brother shot Rory a smug look. "Looks like you'll have your big chance to impress Kristi, bro. Good strategy!"

Both Rory and Kristi argued that wasn't the situation at all. But they really had no choice. A man was in trouble. He could die. Both of them needed to do what they could to save Everett Durfee.

It was simply their nature, and Rory mentally cursed Kristi's unselfishness, which would put her at risk as well.

By radio, Doc Justine let Jane know of their plan.

There had been no change in Everett's condition, which brought a renewed frown to the doctor's forehead.

"The longer he goes without treatment, the greater the damage to his heart could be," she reminded the rescue team.

"I'll pack up the medical equipment we'll need." Kristi's gaze slid to Rory. A slight frown tugged her brows together, her expression more determined than worried. Courageous and unselfish.

"I'll get our cold-weather gear and supplies together," Rory said. "And I promise I'll get you there and bring you back safely. You can count on me."

"I hope so. This time."

She turned and walked toward the examining rooms, leaving Rory wondering what she'd meant by her last remark. Whatever it was, he imagined neither one of them would get much sleep before they had to head out at first light.

DAWN BROUGHT very little illumination to the landscape. The gray light cast few shadows, making it difficult to follow the old roadway. Pine trees and firs were buried until only their snow-laden tips showed above the drifts. If there were any houses in the area, they were invisible beyond the curtain of falling snow. No glimmer of sunrise gave a hint of the direction they were traveling. Without Rory guiding her, Kristi would have been lost a half mile out of town.

She kept her snowmobile in the tracks left by Rory's snowmobile and the sled he was pulling, letting him cut the trail. In addition to the medical equipment she'd gathered together, they'd brought along survival gear, including a rifle strapped onto Rory's machine, which she sincerely hoped he wouldn't have to use against a marauding black bear.

They were bundled up against the weather in so many layers of clothing, it was a wonder either of them could move. Even so, bits of ice and snow crept past zippers and slipped behind her visor, stinging her flesh and threatening to drop her body temperature to dangerous levels. They hadn't gone far before she began to wonder how foolhardy this trip might be.

As long as there was some way to reach Everett Durfee and bring him to safety, her conscience wouldn't have permitted her not to try. But she didn't want to lose her own life in the process. She didn't want to do anything so foolish that she'd deprive Adam of a mother, particularly since he was growing up without a father.

I'll get you there and bring you back safely, Rory had said. Surely this time she could trust his word.

She glanced ahead, beyond the turkey-tail of snow blowing back from Rory's snowmobile. How would he react if he knew the truth? Did she dare risk finding out? Or would that be even more dangerous than this freezing-cold rescue attempt through the woods.

The small radio in her helmet sputtered over the roar of the snowmobile, startling her.

"You okay back there?"

She quickly blocked the fears that had plagued her since she'd made the decision to return to Grass

Valley to help her grandmother—and tell Rory the truth. "I'm mentally planning a trip to Palm Springs when this is all over," she quipped.

"Great. We can get hot together there. Right about now a little slow heat sounds good to me, too."

He'd responded in a low, intimate baritone, and a shudder went through Kristi. This time it wasn't from the cold. They'd been *hot* together that summer she'd fallen in love, hot enough to singe the sheets. And once their fervent lovemaking had nearly melted a scratchy blanket they'd taken on a picnic to a secluded spot near the river.

"Come to think of it," he continued, his disembodied voice caressing her in ways she hadn't been touched in a long time, "I've never seen you in a swimsuit. The one time we went swimming in the river, we omitted that little item of clothing."

The chips of ice that had reached her flesh melted with the heat that flushed her body. "Rory!" She swallowed hard. "Will you hush up. This isn't a private phone line. Somebody could be listening to the radio."

His warm chuckle made her acutely aware of the vibrating snowmobile she was straddling. Her whole body trembled with every motion of the vehicle, and a sensation of warmth formed in the overheated vee between her thighs.

"Not much chance of that, sweetheart. These radios only transmit about a mile. It's just the two of us out here in the woods."

"Well, there *could* be someone listening. I'd just

as soon not give them your version of phone sex to talk about.''

''It'd make their day. I know it's making mine.'' His voice dropped to an even more private note. ''We were great together, Kristi.''

Erotic images flooded her brain—of Rory kissing her, tugging and nipping at her lips. Rory laving her breasts with his tongue. Rory above her blocking out the sun as he entered her for the first time. Rory watching her with his dark, intense eyes as she came apart in his arms. An experience that transcended anything she had imagined could pass between a man and a woman.

She uttered a low, throaty moan.

''Something wrong?''

Oh, yes, everything was wrong—starting with her visit to Grass Valley that fateful summer. She'd only been a vacation fling to him. He'd been so much more to her.

''How do I turn off this blasted radio?'' she asked in panicky retreat.

His laughter careened around her, and her eyes fluttered closed against the deep ache that filled her chest.

Another big mistake, she realized as her snowmobile plowed its way out of the rut Rory's machine had cut through the snow and she nearly stalled the engine before wrenching herself back onto the track.

She needed to concentrate, both on where she was going and on her life. Rory wasn't a part of that picture except as a temporary guide to the Durfee cabin.

A medical emergency had brought her out here, not the urge for a romantic interlude.

By not returning her phone calls, he'd chosen to not become involved with her. He'd found another woman. Yes, Kristi felt guilty about not telling Rory about her pregnancy—about his son. But dammit, she'd tried! And her guilty conscience—and her grandmother's injured ankle—had forced her to confront what she feared most. Rory's rejection of her and her son, and the possibility of a custody battle.

She had a lot at stake here, and her damn reawakened libido had better learn to behave itself.

Determined, she adjusted her position on the snowmobile to ease the pressure and tightened her grip on the throttle. *This* time there'd be no burning up the sheets; she would stay in control of her emotions.

THE SNOWMOBILE SURGED beneath Rory's legs and so did hot blood through his veins.

Had he imagined Kristi's heated response to his teasing words? Did her low, throaty sigh mean she was remembering, too? Did she still want him as much as he wanted her?

The snow blew horizontally toward him, reducing his visibility to almost nothing. He let his instincts guide him, keep him on course. The feel of the terrain. A clue from a fleeting glimpse of cuts in a hillside that had been made when the old dirt road was laid out. The hundreds of hours he'd spent tramping through pine forests and exploring prairie grasslands gave him a sense of the land.

Navigating through a blizzard was a helluva lot

easier than knowing what Kristi was thinking. One mistake with her and he'd be over the side of the road in an instant, his second chance lost.

But did he really have a second chance with a self-proclaimed city girl? Maybe Grass Valley wouldn't be enough for her now.

Maybe he'd *never* been enough for her and that's why she'd never written. Never called.

Clearing the negative thoughts from his mind, he spoke into his helmet microphone. "How are your feet doing?"

"What feet?"

His lips quirked. Despite the cold she was hanging on to her sense of humor. "I'm going to look for a place out of the wind to pull over. We need to get our circulation back."

"Wonderful. Maybe there's a four-star hotel over the next hill."

He chuckled. "I'll check my tour book."

Within a quarter mile they rounded a bend in the road that was edged with a sheltered stand of pines heavily laden with snow. He eased the snowmobile in that direction and pulled to a halt, turning off the engine. Kristi followed him into the copse of trees.

Dismounting, he shrugged out of his backpack. In order to get at the contents, he had to shed his heavy snow gloves.

"Stomp your feet and walk around some," he directed Kristi as she climbed off her shiny blue vehicle. Encased in the thick garb of a recreational snowmobiler, she looked like a delectable snowlady who'd had a helmet plopped on her head. Rory had the urge to uncover what was beneath those layers of fabric and insulation, garment by garment. Probably not a good idea with the temperature about twenty-five degrees and the windchill factor around zero.

He uncapped the thermos he'd taken from his backpack. "Hot chocolate whenever you're ready," he announced. "It'll warm you from the inside out."

She shifted her helmet toward the back of her head and reached for the thermos top he'd filled with the steaming beverage. "My insides aren't the problem, but I could use a hot tub to stick my feet in."

"Hot tubs are good. You still like to swim naked? Or have you become the modest type?"

Her head snapped up, and she sloshed hot chocolate over her gloved hand. "Since I've never been in a hot tub, I have no idea how I would like it."

"Too bad we aren't closer to Yellowstone. We could slip into one of those bubbling pools—"

"I think the Durfees would be happier if we just did what we came to do and get Everett to a hospital as soon as we can."

He lifted one shoulder in an indolent shrug that was a sham. He cared too much about Kristi to be unaffected by her brusque tone. "A guy can dream, can't he?"

"Not when the life of someone else is at stake. Or their future."

Rory sensed she was talking about something besides the current medical crisis, but he wasn't all that good at reading women. In college he hadn't had much time for dating; he'd been lashed to the books with only a faint hope he would manage to finish the rigorous training to become a vet. Since then, living in Grass Valley, the selection of females had been limited. Granted, he'd dated a few women but none of them had clicked.

No woman could compare to his memories of Kristi.

She drained the cup and passed it back to him. "Thanks."

"You're welcome." Their words sounded too formal, considering all that they had once shared together.

He filled the cup again and sipped while keeping his gaze on Kristi. Her cheeks were flushed with the cold, twin spots the color of a summer rose. Her eyes were almost midnight blue under the cloudy sky, and their depths held both question and pride. "Don't mess with me" radiated from the way she held her shoulders so rigidly.

"Should we be moving on?" she asked.

"Can you feel your feet again?"

"Warm as toast."

He didn't believe that for a moment but he didn't see any point in arguing.

Returning the capped thermos to the backpack, he risked unzipping his heavy jacket long enough to pull out his cell phone.

"Who are you calling?"

"Thought I'd get a weather report from my brother." He flipped open the phone, switched it on and waited for something to happen. *Nada.*

"You can't get a connection?"

"Nope. This far north the coverage is inconsistent

under the best of circumstances. With this storm, I didn't think there'd be much of a chance. We'll have to wait till we get to the Durfees' radio.''

"My best guess is that the report calls for continued snow and intermittent freezing toes. I think we'd better keep going." She pulled her helmet down again, tapped the visor into place, turned and walked back to her snowmobile.

Intermittent was right, as far as her reactions to him were concerned. One minute she was bright, witty or moaning into the radio headset in her helmet. The next thing he knew, she was all bristle like a porcupine under attack.

God, he'd never understand women!

THE CLOUDS BEGAN to lift and with them the snow turned to big, fluffy flakes, falling more gently to the ground. Even so, it seemed an eternity before a small cabin loomed ahead of them in a clearing. Sturdily made of hand-hewn logs, a faint trace of smoke drifted from a chimney, but no lights shone from the windows that sat on either side of the door.

Rory pulled his snowmobile to a stop in front of the porch, which was a foot or two below the current snow level. Someone had shoveled a path partway around to the side of the house. No doubt Everett's nearly fatal project.

Beyond the path were two sets of footprints sinking deeply into the snow.

"Thank goodness we're finally here," Kristi said as she parked next to Rory and dismounted, stomping her feet in the futile hope of regaining her circulation.

The thought of having to get back on the snowmobile for the return trip filled her with shivery dread. She'd never be warm again.

After the racket of the snowmobiles, the clearing was eerily still. Snowflakes drifted down soundlessly, creating a blanket of silence. Kristi heard only the tick of cooling engines and the soft hum of pine needles shifting under the press of snow.

"I'm surprised Jane hasn't come out to greet us," she whispered, unwilling to break the quiet of the clearing. "She had to have heard us coming."

"Maybe she's occupied with Everett." Rory walked up to the door and knocked. Wearing heavy cold-weather gear, including moon boots, he looked a bit like a traveler from outer space. Yet he moved with the smooth strides of a born athlete, totally confident, no wasted motions.

He'd been like that as a lover, too. Confident. Masterful. Each stroke designed to arouse and give pleasure.

When he knocked again and still got no answer, Kristi said, "I've got a bad feeling about this. Maybe something has happened to Jane, too."

Testing the latch, he found the door unlocked, probably not unusual in this remote part of the world but still troubling from Kristi's point of view. Jane really should have greeted them by now.

He shoved the door open and called to the cabin's occupants. "Jane? Everett? It's Rory Oakes. Are you here?" When he got no response he stepped inside.

With images of the couple succumbing to carbon

monoxide from the wood fire or freezing to death in their isolated world, Kristi followed him inside.

The cozy living area featured a comfortable-appearing couch with a colorful afghan tossed over the back and a wooden rocking chair. Books cluttered several pine shelves, and skeins of yarn spilled out of a basket beside the rocking chair, the work-in-progress draped over its arm. Nearby a potbellied wood stove provided heat for the cabin.

At the opposite end of the dimly lit room stood the kitchen and eating area. Except for a mug on the counter, everything was neat and tidy, including the radio on a table by the wall. Kerosene lanterns were placed around the room at various locations.

Rory peered into the adjacent room. "Nobody's here."

Worried, Kristi glanced around. "Where could they be?"

"I haven't a clue." His dark brows tugged together. "Put a couple more logs in the fire. I'll go around back and crank up the generator. Maybe Jane radioed Eric to let him know what was going on."

"Do you think something's happened to them?"

"I think Jane has her head on straight. They've lived remotely for a dozen years or more. Wherever they are, I'd put my money on them to survive."

Kristi hoped so. It hardly seemed possible someone came along and did them harm, not in this weather. But a wife desperate to save her husband's life might do something foolish.

Pulling off her heavy gloves and peeling off her snowsuit, Kristi added fuel from the wood box to the banked fire. The Durfees hadn't been gone long. The temperature in the cabin was well above freezing.

The low roar of the generator kicked in, filling the unnatural silence in the cabin. Moments later Rory returned, stomping the snow from his boots and slapping his gloves together. Tugging off his ski cap, he shook his head, shifting the strands of his midnight-black hair back into place.

"They've gone off on their tractor," he announced.

"Jane and Everett?"

He nodded.

"Why didn't they wait for us?" If they were planning to leave on their own, they sure could have saved Rory and Kristi a long, uncomfortable trip.

"Who knows." He shrugged out of his gear, tossed it aside and went to the radio, switching it on.

"They could have at least left a note so we'd know what was going on." Not that a note would have changed anything. She and Rory still would have endured that miserably cold ride.

"Maybe they let Eric or the doc know what was up."

It didn't take long for Eric to respond to Rory's call on the emergency radio frequency.

"I gather you made it to the Durfees' cabin."

"We did," Rory responded, speaking into a small black microphone with a curling cord stretching to the radio. The dials glowed orange in the half light of a midday twilight. "But there's nobody here except us snow bunnies. Did Jane check in with you before taking off?'' He paused a moment, then Eric responded.

"Right. She radioed shortly after you left. I tried your cell phone but you were out of range." Rory nodded at that comment. "Everett regained consciousness. Jane thought she'd detected a break in the weather and decided to bring him in herself. They took the tractor down the river route, arrived about a half hour ago. They brought their dog along, too, so you've got the cabin to yourself."

"A dog?" Rory asked.

"A big Lab. He's big enough they both could have ridden him into town if their tractor had broken down."

Kristi silently groaned. She and Rory had wasted the trip and half frozen their buns off in the process. "Ask how Everett is doing."

Eric reported the patient was resting under Doc Justine's care, but they weren't sure when they'd be able to transport him to Great Falls. "The snow is still falling like crazy here—there'll be another foot or more of snow on the ground by suppertime. Most of the power lines are down and the phones are out."

Rory shoved his fingers through his hair. "Okay. We're going to get warmed up, then we'll be heading back."

"I wouldn't do that, bro."

Frowning, Rory glanced at Kristi, his eyes worried. "Why wouldn't we?" he asked into the microphone.

"The weather is deteriorating. A second storm is coming in on top of the first. They're expecting heavier than usual snowfall all along the Canadian border.

Nothing is going to be moving in this part of the country for the next two days, minimum.''

Kristi gasped. ''Two days?''

The intensity of Rory's gaze deepened, holding Kristi's with a sensual power, and she couldn't look away. ''Are you sure, White Eyes?'' he asked his brother.

''Positive. We're going to have a mess here in Grass Valley, and it'll be worse where you are. You'll have to shovel the snow off the roof and keep a path open to the generator. If I were you, I'd stick right where you are till this blows over.''

''Understood,'' he said, his voice husky, his gaze never leaving Kristi's face. ''We'll stay put till you give us the all clear.''

''Good luck.''

Good luck? Kristi's stomach sank, and her heart followed it down.

My God, this was the worst possible misfortune she could imagine.

Suddenly the heat from the potbellied stove scorched her back. She was stranded in a remote cabin and would be for days.

With Rory...the one man she was afraid to face with the truth.

Chapter Four

Rory switched off the radio, but his gaze lingered on Kristi. Wanting her. Hungry for what they had once had together.

The red highlights in her hair seemed to dance in the muted light, bright and shiny—inviting—in contrast to the wary look in her eyes.

"You're not afraid to stay with me in the cabin, are you?" he asked.

"Afraid? In what way?"

He placed the radio mike on the table and walked toward her. "You tell me."

She retreated a step. "I'm just a little anxious to get back to town. I'm supposed to be helping Justine at the clinic. She has a seriously ill patient on her hands, and she's not very mobile."

"Eric's trained in emergency first aid. He'll fill in for you."

The way she glanced around the cabin, she reminded Rory of a frightened doe about to bolt. "A heart patient needs more than a little first aid."

"There's not much we can do about it now, not with the weather closing in on us again."

As though to emphasize his point, a howling gust of wind rattled the windows, and pelting snow piled up on the ledge. In response, wood crackled in the stove.

Kristi visibly shivered and hugged her arms together. "I know we can't leave. I just hadn't expected to be stranded—"

"With me?" His lips quirked. "Strikes me as a perfect opportunity for us to get reacquainted. I'm sure there's plenty of food, and I saw a couple of cords of wood out back. We'll be as cozy as a couple of lovebirds in a cage."

"Well, I for one don't feel cozy and we *aren't* lovebirds. You can get that thought out of your head right now."

She was as bristly as a mother bear after a winter's hibernation, and Rory wasn't sure why. "Look, if you've got a boyfriend in Spokane, and you're worried he'll be upset that we got stuck here together, I'm sure—"

"I don't have a boyfriend."

"Then what's bothering you? You act like you're mad at me about something."

Kristi opened her mouth to speak, to tell him the truth, then whirled away to look out the window at the swirling snow, as wild as her own spiraling emotions. The words she needed to say clogged her throat so tightly she could barely breathe.

She had no idea how he would react to the news that he had a son. He might be furious with her. Or he might deny Adam was his son, rejecting the boy sight unseen. Or he might demand full custody as a way to punish her for keeping the boy from him all these years.

Whatever his reaction, she'd have to endure three days of living in close proximity to the man. No way to escape. Nowhere to hide from the storm of his emotions—or hers—that would follow her revelation.

Her emotions were likely to be as volatile as his. Ever since she realized Rory wasn't going to call her, she'd kept her feelings of anger and betrayal bottled inside. He'd found someone else, the woman on the phone had told Kristi. As far as he was concerned, Kristi and her baby were on their own.

Once she let the truth out of that snug little spot where she'd been keeping it, there'd be no holding her emotions in check. The knot of pain she'd carried near her heart all these years would burst in a torrent of accusations and bitterness. She couldn't let that happen. Not yet. Not until she knew what kind of man Rory had become—and if she had the strength to go on no matter what his feelings might be for her and her son.

"Kristi, I can't fix whatever is bothering you unless you tell me what's wrong."

She closed her eyes and drew in a steadying breath before turning to face him again. In the shadows he looked impossibly big and tall, his dark hair sliding across his strong forehead. She'd always loved brushing it back into place, though it had a will of its own, never remaining there for long. She had an urge to repeat that futile gesture now and clenched her fists against the impulse.

His coal-black eyes studied her from across the room. "I promise nothing is going to happen between us, Kristi, that you don't want to happen. You're safe with me."

She'd never been *safe* with Rory. When she'd visited Grass Valley that summer, she'd been too young, too in love, to recognize that. She was older and wiser now, and had more at stake.

"Since we're stuck here, we might as well make the best of it." She picked up her jacket from the chair where she'd dropped it. "I'll start bringing our gear inside—"

"I'll get the gear and put the snowmobiles in the shed out back. No need for us both to freeze our rear ends off again. You can see if there are makings for coffee."

She lifted her brows in question as he pulled on his heavy gloves. "Am I to take it you believe the kitchen is exclusively the domain of all us frail women?"

"Nope. If you want to do the cold work, I can handle the coffee. I make a pretty mean omelet, too." His grin was downright devilish as he set his gloves aside and unzipped his jacket. "Of course, after I got the vehicles put away I was going to shovel some of the snow off the roof so it doesn't collapse and make sure the chimney is clear. Then I was planning to bring in some more wood for the fire. But I don't mind enjoying a leisurely cup of java while you take care of all that."

"A true gentleman."

"Yep. That's me." In a gesture so familiar that it made her ache with longing, he brushed his hair back from his forehead.

She swallowed hard and licked her lips. "Perhaps in the interest of equal opportunity for frostbite, we should share the workload. From what I've heard about Jane Durfee, there're probably two shovels lying around somewhere."

His smile broadened. "Your wish is my command."

Once upon a time she'd wished that he would love her. Love the child they'd created together. Marry her and live happily ever after. That every night he would hold her and kiss her, and in the morning he'd do it again until her endless desire for him was sated.

Now she was going to shovel three feet of snow off the roof with him and hope neither of them would break their respective necks.

Not exactly the future she had once longed for.

MORE THAN ONCE, Kristi's mother had told her she was stubborn to a fault. Now she believed her mom.

She'd helped to carry their gear into the cabin, drag the snowmobiles into the shed, haul wood and was now standing precariously on top of the cabin's roof barely able to keep her footing. And she was cold. Really cold. The snow blew past her at forty miles per hour, battering her face and lowering visibility to almost nothing. If she'd had any sense, she would have let Rory play macho man and do all this outside work on his own.

But no, she had to be *stubborn*.

If he was going to work outside in a blizzard, risking frostbite or worse, then so would she. That way she wouldn't be obligated to him. They'd be on an equal footing. She wouldn't have to tell him what a wonderful man he was, how strong and determined.

Nor would she have to admit to herself, after years of carrying the burden of single parenthood, she'd love to be able to lean on him.

Or so she'd rationalized an hour ago before her feet had become totally numb and she could no longer feel her fingers. In contrast, sweat edged down between her breasts from all the exertion. If she stopped shoveling for more than a moment she'd be chilled to the bone.

She'd almost finished clearing her side of the roof, and she slid her shovel into another mound of snow, giving it a shove. Her boots slipped on the icy shingles. Trying to keep her balance, she pinwheeled her arms in the air. She lost her grip on the shovel, and it went sliding off the roof. Unable to stop her own momentum, she went slipping and sliding after the shovel.

"Help!" she screamed.

"Kristi!" Rory bellowed.

She fell on her back with a poof into a snowdrift behind the cabin. The wind left her lungs in a rush, and she looked up just in time to see a cascade of snow following her down. Then the gray, snow-laden sky vanished into darkness.

Rory leaped from the roof, driven by a fear more powerful than he'd ever before experienced. He landed thigh deep in the snow near where Kristi had fallen and struggled toward her. His heart was in his throat, his stomach wrenched into a knot. She could be badly injured. Broken bones. A concussion.

Dammit! He should have made her stay in Grass Valley.

Frantically he swept away the snow that covered her. Her face was nearly as white as the snow, her eyes glazed. "Kristi. Talk to me, sweetheart." *God, don't let her die.*

He tugged off his glove to take her pulse and lowered his head toward her face to check her breathing.

She coughed. "Can't…"

Relief, so potent it drained the blood from his head, swept through him. *She was alive.* "It's okay. You've had the wind knocked out of you. Give it a second."

Sitting back on his haunches, he continued to stroke her face, wiping away bits of snow and ice, cherishing the smooth feel of her skin no matter how chilled it was.

"Can you move your hands and arms?" he asked.

She did, and he nodded.

"What about your legs?"

She moved enough for him to know she didn't have a serious neck or back injury, and he sent up a prayer of thanks.

"Do you hurt anywhere? Any broken bones?"

"I don't think so," she whispered. "I'm cold."

"Okay. We'll take care of that right away." He glanced around through the swirling snow to get his bearings and to plan the best route to the front of the cabin. He wished he had a back board and someone to help him carry Kristi inside. But that wasn't the case, and right now she needed to be in out of the cold.

Crouching beside her, he lifted her in his arms. Since she'd come back to town, he'd wanted to hold her close to him. But not like this. Not when she might be injured and at risk for frostbite.

Even so, when he caught the faint hint of her apple-scented shampoo he reacted as though the heat of summer had suddenly surrounded him, bringing with it the scent and the memories of Kristi in his arms. He'd once carried her out of the river where they'd been swimming and placed her on a blanket in the shade. There, one by one, he'd licked away the drops of water that had clung to her. Tasted her feminine flavor along with the fresh, clear water. Finally he'd loved her, possessing her.

In return, she had possessed him.

Kristi's arms circled his neck as he stumbled through the deep snow.

"You're going to hurt yourself trying to carry me," she said. "I think I can walk."

"I like having you right where you are." The memories and his need for her made his voice husky with wanting.

She shivered, and he wasn't sure if it was a reaction to his words or to the cold.

He reached the porch and made it up the stairs. Adjusting his grip, he flipped the latch and carried her inside. The relative warmth radiating from the potbellied stove enveloped them.

He managed to ease her down to the couch before she started shivering in earnest.

"We've got to get you out of that snowsuit and warmed up," he said, pulling off his heavy gloves and tossing them aside.

"I'll be f-fine," she stammered.

He tugged off her snow cap, letting her red-gold hair tumble free. "No breaks or bruises we need to worry about?"

She shook her head, but her fingers trembled wildly as she tried to work the zipper on her jacket.

"I'll get that."

She tried to push his hands away. "I c-can manage."

He ignored her comment, brushing away the snow that had lodged in the zipper and helping her out of her jacket. She wore a heavy wool sweater beneath it. The neck and hem were edged with ice crystals.

"The sweater has to come off, too," he told her.

"Rory, I am not going to sit around here in my—"

He pulled off her sweater, revealing her longjohn top, a soft flannel in pale blue. Another time he might have taken advantage of the situation, caressing the fleecy fabric and exploring the feminine contours the top so vividly outlined. But for now his only goal was to stop the shivers that shook her body.

He should have made her stay inside while he took care of the roof.

"I'll get you a blanket to wrap up in in a minute." He tugged a colorful afghan from the back of the couch and draped it around her shoulders, pulling it tight.

"You didn't used to be so b-bossy," she stammered.

"Sure I was. You just didn't notice because the rest of my personality is so charming."

She snorted something unintelligible.

Her boots didn't come off easily. Snow had gotten packed inside, and her feet stuck. He had to straddle her leg backward to tug the boots free.

When he finally got rid of both boots, she groaned and her teeth chattered. "My feet are so c-cold."

Pulling off her heavy socks, he tried to rub some life back into her feet. The tips of her toes were white, and he knew she'd been close to frostbite. He cursed himself for being so careless with her well-being.

Over her objections, he managed to get her heavy snow pants off and brought her a thick quilt from the bedroom. "Wrap up good, and I'll bring you some warm water to soak your feet in."

"I don't need—"

"You used to be better at listening to what I said."

"Maybe I was so young and naive, I trusted you more then than I should have."

"Trust me now, babe. Your toes are on the verge of frostbite, and if we don't warm them up, you could be in serious trouble."

Kristi scowled at him but didn't offer any further argument. How could she? She knew he was right. She was shaking so hard her teeth were chattering. Gooseflesh covered her whole body. If Rory hadn't been there to help her when the snow had buried her, she could easily have succumbed to hypothermia. Assuming she hadn't died of asphyxiation first.

Of course, if she hadn't been trying to prove she was as strong and determined as Rory, she wouldn't be in this fix in the first place.

But sitting on the couch wrapped in a quilt, she felt vulnerable. Her longjohns were modest, covering her from throat to ankle, but they were also revealing. Her every curve showed, every fault in her figure, including the swell of her stomach that she'd never been able to rid herself of since Adam's birth.

Minutes later she girded herself as he returned with a pail of water he'd heated on the stove. He was being so damn nice! It wasn't fair when she didn't want to care about him again.

"I warmed the water just a little," he said. "But it's still likely to hurt when you put your feet in the pail."

He cupped her calf with his palm and lifted her leg. She wanted to tell him she'd do it on her own, that she didn't want him touching her. Didn't want the feel of his hand caressing her. Didn't want to see the fan of his eyelashes as he knelt in front of her, or be tempted to brush back the dark lock of hair from his forehead.

Didn't want to fight the desperate urge to ask him to hold her again.

She winced as he gently slipped first one foot and then the other into the water. A thousand sharp knives pricked her toes and the bottoms of her feet. But the tears that sprang to her eyes were about another kind of pain, one that cried out from her heart.

"It'll be better in a minute, hon. Hang on." He soothed his palms over her calves, warming her in ways that only he had been able to do.

Closing her eyes, she gritted her teeth and tried to block the memories that rose in her mind. Rory rubbing her ankle when she'd twisted it scrambling up a rocky hillside wearing tennis shoes. The way he'd looked up at her, his eyes dilated with arousal. His kiss, their first, and how their lips had seemed to fit together as though they'd been made for each other.

She tugged her lip between her teeth to prevent a moan from escaping. Years had passed and still the memory was so vivid it was as though that kiss had happened yesterday. Or only moments ago.

"You've stopped shivering," he said in a low, raspy voice. "That's good."

She opened her eyes to find him looking at her with that same heated look she remembered so clearly. But this time he wasn't going to kiss her. She wouldn't let him. She didn't dare because she was sure she'd never want him to stop.

Straightening her shoulders, she tugged the quilt more firmly around her. "How is it you didn't get as cold as I did?" *How could you not have been as affected by our relationship as I was?*

He eased back onto his haunches. "For one thing, I didn't try to bury myself in six feet of snow."

"I didn't exactly plan it that way." She'd never intended to fall in love with Rory or anyone else that summer. She'd had her future all sketched out. Rory—and the baby she'd conceived with him—had changed everything.

He grinned. "For another, I'm bigger and tougher than you are and more used to cold weather."

"Apparently, you're not as foolish as I am, either." He hadn't lost his heart as completely that summer as she had, and he had been able to move on with his life. Which is more than she could say for herself. It had taken her months to paste the pieces of her heart back together when she finally acknowledged she would never hear from Rory again. Each day had dragged into the next with her only having enough energy to deal with the necessities.

Then suddenly, as if by some miracle, she had a baby she loved more than she'd ever thought possible and he needed her to be strong. She'd done her best from then on, only faltering when it came to telling Rory he had a son.

She still lacked the courage to take that dangerous step.

Standing, Rory said, "Keep soaking your feet until the water starts to feel cold. Meanwhile, I'll make us some hot chocolate. I could use a little warming up myself."

A shiver that had nothing to do with her icy experience sped down Kristi's spine. How on earth would she ever find the *right* time to tell Rory the truth? Was it already too late?

FOR SUPPER, Rory raided the Durfees' pantry for a couple of cans of chili con carne and made a dozen biscuits from a mix. The wood stove's oven didn't heat evenly, burning the edges of the biscuits and leaving the centers doughy. Which wasn't about to stop either Rory or Kristi from consuming their fair share. It had been a long, hard day spent mostly in below-freezing weather. They'd consumed a lot of calories trying to stay warm.

"You certainly know your way around the kitchen," Kristi commented as she scraped off a little charcoal from the biscuit she'd selected.

Rory found himself admiring her outfit, although on anyone else it wouldn't look nearly so sexy. She'd found one of Jane's flannel shirts in the bedroom and was wearing that along with a pair of jeans about three sizes too big. One of Everett's belts pulled tight around her slender waist provided the faint hope that the jeans would stay where she wanted them.

"A lifelong bachelor learns to appreciate gourmet meals like this," he said with a wry grin.

She arched eyebrows the same shade as her strawberry-blond hair. "So you've never married?"

"Nope. Not many choices around Grass Valley." He spooned some chili into his mouth to get rid of the taste of burned dough. "In all honesty, since I graduated, I've been pretty busy getting my vet practice going and trying to pay off my student loans and the mortgage on my place."

"I was lucky that Grandma was willing to pay for most of my education."

"But you decided against going to med school?"

"Nursing is a perfectly good career." She made a production out of spreading strawberry jam on her biscuit as though she wanted to avoid looking at him.

"But you wanted to be a doctor. A pediatrician."

"I changed my mind, okay?" Her gaze snapped across the table, sending the message that the subject was at an end. "How about your brothers? Are they married yet?"

Rory decided not to pursue the issue, for now. "Eric hasn't taken the big plunge yet, but Walker got married about six months ago. He and Lizzie have a year-old daughter, Susie-Q. As cute and cuddly as a kitten. Well, not that fuzzy, of course."

Kristi lifted her brows again. "A year old?"

"It's a little complicated. Lizzie was going to marry someone else—that was after Susie's biological father had died. But Lizzie decided she didn't love the new guy and ran away a couple of days before the wedding. She showed up on Walker's doorstep claiming to be his new housekeeper."

"That took a lot of spunk."

The flame in the kerosene lantern hanging above the kitchen table flickered in response to a gust of wind that had sneaked inside the cabin from the storm, shifting the shadows that fell across Kristi's face. To conserve gasoline, Rory had turned off the generator when they'd gone outside to shovel the roof.

"Lizzie's all right—for a city girl," Rory said. "And Walker's pretty much head over heels for her."

"I gather you don't care for city girls?"

"You can see for yourself that living this far north isn't an easy thing to do."

"Meaning only big macho guys like you can survive here?"

His brows tugged together. What the heck was Kristi getting all bristly about now? "Lizzie seems to be doing okay. She made it through the winter, anyway."

"Three cheers for her." With more enthusiasm than appeared necessary, Kristi scraped the bottom of her bowl clean.

"There's more chili if you want some."

"I'm fine. Thank you."

In that case Rory decided to help himself to what was left in the pot. That might give him a chance to figure out what was bugging Kristi. Although, he didn't think he was that clever. She'd been all over the map emotionally since she arrived in Grass Valley. Hard to know what she was thinking.

At the stove, he dished up the rest of the chili and stood there with his back to the fire watching Kristi as he ate a few bites. It seemed to him things were a lot simpler six years ago. He wanted her; she wanted him. *Bingo.* Clearly things had changed.

"Walker and Lizzie also adopted four teenage boys Walker had had as foster kids for the past few years, plus one of their younger sisters," Rory said, trying to fill the silence. "It was a nice payback for our dad having put up with us. But it also means they've got a pretty big family already, and they haven't even started on their own kids yet."

She ran her fingertip over an uneven plank of the hand-hewn table. "Big families are nice. I hated being an only child."

"But you're not married. There's no guy waiting for you back in Spokane?"

"No."

He moved away from the stove and lowered his voice. "In that case, I'd say the men in Spokane are either blind or damn fools."

Color bloomed in her cheeks, her fair complexion giving away her embarrassment. Rory marveled that she didn't seem to realize how beautiful she was, how genuinely lovely. Or how much a man could want her.

Picking up her dish, she shoved her chair back from the table and stood. "Since you fixed dinner, I'll do the dishes."

"There aren't that many. We could do them together, like a team, huh?"

She nailed him with a look that didn't bode well for the outcome of any game he wanted to play.

"Thanks, anyway. I'd rather do it myself." She marched to the sink and began to use the hand pump to fill the pail to heat more water. "Why don't you check with Eric on the radio? Maybe there's been a change in the weather."

Rory didn't think there was much chance of that. Not from the way the wind was howling outside or how frigid the air in the cabin had become. And Kristi's attitude had created a virtual wall of ice between them.

He could only hope in the next forty-eight hours or so, before the storm wore itself out, he'd be able to find a way to melt that ice.

Meanwhile he'd have to trudge around to the back of the cabin again and turn on the generator.

Chapter Five

Kristi rolled up the sleeves of the flannel shirt she'd borrowed from Jane Durfee's closet and dipped her hands into the sudsy water in the dishpan. The warmth felt good in contrast to the icy cold that squeezed her heart. It hurt that Rory had rejected the love she'd been so willing to offer him yet talked so fondly about his brother's happiness.

Behind her, Rory was talking with Eric on the radio. The weather news didn't sound good.

"We had to bring the Snodgrass family into the church shelter," Eric said, his voice oddly tinny over the radio. "Half of the roof on their house fell in. They had to send their oldest girl, Sherri, into town for help."

"Probably because her father was too drunk to go himself," Rory muttered as Eric continued to relate the problems the storm was causing in Grass Valley.

"Ginger Laity's baby decided to arrive a little early. She couldn't get into town, so Pete delivered the baby on his own. Then he fainted and hit his head on the floor. Ginger had to put him to bed for the rest of the day.''

Kristi smiled to herself. She'd worked labor and delivery enough to know some of the strongest men couldn't handle the sight of blood. And when it was their wife's blood, a smart nurse kept an ampule of ammonia handy.

She shot a glance at Rory. He was more than capable of handling an emergency and, as a veterinarian, blood didn't bother him. But she couldn't help wondering how he would have reacted during her delivery. She could have used his strong, steady hand to hold on to.

Regret tightened in her chest along with residual anger that he hadn't been there for her.

Walker continued relaying news of town. ''Doc Justine sends her best to Kristi and promises she's staying off her feet. Folks are keeping close to home in this storm. Except for the Laitys, nobody's had a medical crisis. She figures there'll be a run on the clinic when the weather clears.''

Forcefully tamping down her emotions, Kristi nodded. Grandma Justine would need her after the storm passed.

''How about Walker?'' Rory asked when Eric broke for a response. ''How are things out at the ranch?''

''The ranch house is all buttoned up, but he and his boys have been out looking for any cows that dropped their calves early. That's their biggest worry.''

''Searching for newborn calves in a blizzard is

miserable work. Sorry I can't be there to help him out." He didn't sound entirely sincere as he glanced at Kristi. Their eyes met, held for a moment before he smiled and she looked away. "So how much longer is this storm going to last?"

"The weatherman says we're looking at another thirty-six to forty-eight hours before it clears out of here. At least, if you have to be snowbound, you've got great company in Kristi. Enjoy yourself." Eric's chuckle blended with the static on the radio.

"Yeah," Rory responded softly. "That sounds like a good plan to me. A lot better than rounding up stray cows and their offspring."

An unwelcome surge of sexual awareness swirled through Kristi's midsection. Their isolation couldn't be more complete or more rife with temptation. Kristi had once succumbed to that temptation. She didn't dare repeat the same mistake.

Rory had failed her. Nowhere was it written that he wouldn't do it again.

Kristi snatched up a drying cloth to wipe the few dishes she had washed. The next two days were likely to be among the most difficult of her life.

She finished up the dishes, put them away and made a point of finding a paperback to read by the time Rory switched off the radio and went outside to turn off the generator. The kerosene lamps would provide what light they needed, the potbellied stove all the heat they could use.

The wind was still howling outside as she settled into the rocking chair near the potbellied stove. Only when she opened the book did she realize it was a steamy romance. Definitely the wrong selection for her evening's reading pleasure. No way did she want to get into the mood.

Rory planted himself on the couch, stretching out his long legs, crossing them at his ankles. He'd left his boots by the door, and she noticed there was a hole in the toe of his wool sock. He shouldn't be out stomping around in this weather with a hole in his sock, for heaven's sake! He needed a wife to take care of—

Kristi jerked her thoughts back to the book, and she read the same paragraph she'd already read three times. The description of the hero as blond and blue-eyed held little appeal. She was into dark and dangerous—to her regret.

With an effort, she managed to stifle a groan.

"Hey, look at that." Rory popped up from the couch and headed for the bookcase. "The Durfees have got a bunch of games."

When she didn't respond, he rummaged around and pulled out a tattered box. "Monopoly. With any luck, this ought to last us until the storm moves on. Let's play." He carried the box to the kitchen table.

"No, I'd rather read." Actually, she'd rather be back in Grass Valley helping her grandmother treat her patient. Or better yet, home in Spokane with her son. She missed Adam already and had only been away for two days.

"Come on. I'll even let you win."

She eyed him across the room, trying to be unmoved by his boyish grin. "Why is it that I don't believe you?"

"Because I'm a guy?"

Exhaling in defeat, she nodded. "That sounds like a pretty good reason to me." Under the circumstances, playing Monopoly had to be a better choice than reading a sensual romance.

They set up the game board on the table and counted out the money. He even let her be the banker. Which didn't mean he'd give her a discount on the rent of any property he owned, as she soon discovered.

He neatly stacked her rent money on top of his own stash, then rolled the dice, got doubles, landed on a Utility, bought it and rolled again.

"You used to be pretty close to your grandmother, but it seems to me you haven't visited in the past couple of years." This time he drew a "Get Out of Jail Free" card, which he set aside.

"Just like you, I've been busy getting my life in order." *And raising your son.* "Grandma visits us in Spokane a couple of times a year." Justine had made it a point to be there when Kristi's baby was due. Thank heavens! Kristi had unexpectedly hemorrhaged, and only Justine's quick work had saved both Kristi and Adam.

"Guess your mother never liked living here," Rory commented.

"She left when she was nineteen to go to college and never looked back. She hated living in such a small town."

"Some women are like that."

"Men, too. Dad didn't even like to visit. When I was little I used to plead with Mother to let me come see Grandma. I loved the smell of her clinic and see-ing all those people who asked her for help. By the time I was a teenager, it got harder to drop everything to come here for a visit. But by then I was already hooked on a career in medicine.''

''It's also why I never saw you running around town in pigtails.''

''I never wore pigtails,'' she insisted. ''But I did wear braces. And my freckles were terrible in the summer if I spent a lot of time out in the sun. They still are, for that matter.''

He reached across the table and ran his fingertip down her nose in a quick caress. ''Fortunately I hap-pen to like freckles anytime of the year.''

Heat raced to her cheeks, and she jerked away from him, feigning interest in the game board. It wasn't fair that such a simple touch could affect her so strongly. By now she should be immune to what-ever Rory did to her.

Unfortunately, that wasn't the case.

In their next set of turns, Rory bought Connecticut and she landed on Jail.

''I'll sell you my 'Get Out of Jail Free' card,'' he offered.

She eyed the board and his growing investments in property. It seemed unlikely she'd beat him at this game or any other. ''I'll pay the fine, thanks.''

''You remember when the doc taught us how to give injections to an orange?'' he said idly as she spent fifty dollars to bail herself out of jail.

In spite of herself, Kristi smiled at the memory. ''Those poor oranges were the most bruised things around. Still, when I had to demonstrate my skill in nursing school, I got an A plus.''

''Hey, me, too—in vet school, that is.'' He laughed, rolled the dice and bought some more property.

''You've turned into quite a capitalist, Dr. Oakes.''

''All us savages took lessons from the white eyes.''

Rory wasn't a savage at all, except that he had once broken her heart. He was the most gentle man she'd ever known, which is one of the reasons he'd wanted to become a veterinarian. He couldn't bear to see an injured animal. Wounding a woman appeared to be a different matter.

Slowly the game began to even out, though Rory still had more cash than Kristi did. She had more houses, and he added a hotel to his assets.

Outside the wind continued to rattle the windows, and from time to time Rory added wood to the fire.

''I'll have to bring in more wood before we go to bed.''

Bed. Now there was a dilemma they hadn't begun to discuss. There was only one bed. In Kristi's view, it wasn't nearly big enough for the two of them.

''I'll sleep on the couch,'' she quickly volunteered.

He cocked his dark brows, his expression amused. ''So you want to hog all the heat from the stove, huh?''

''No, that's not what I—''

''I mean, I was going to be generous and let you sleep on the couch, anyway, while I slept in the cold

bedroom. I can always use my Arctic sleeping bag
to keep warm. It'll handle temperatures below zero.''

"The bedroom won't be that cold if we leave the
door open.''

"Hmm. I suppose you're right.'' He scratched his
head, apparently surprised by that possibility. ''In
that case, why don't you take the bed and I'll sleep
on the couch? You'll be more comfortable.''

"Rory—''

"I'm not going to cross the threshold to the bedroom whether the door is open or not. That's a promise. Unless you give me the go-ahead, of course.''

She had the distinct impression she was being
bamboozled and sweet-talked at the same time. If she
didn't watch herself, she'd fall for his line all over
again.

Thoughtfully, she rolled the dice and came up doubles. ''That's very kind of you to let me have the
bed. As far as access is concerned, I feel honor-bound
to point out the indoor facilities are accessible only
through the bedroom.'' She landed on Chance and
drew a card.

"Ah, then I hope you won't mind a late night visit
or two.''

Go to Jail. She groaned. ''Only for approved pur-
poses.''

His wickedly sexy smile suggested he wasn't
likely to be bound by her rules.

It didn't take long after that for Kristi to begin
yawning. They had been up since before dawn, and
her body was beginning to reach its limit of endur-

ance. Especially since she'd nearly frozen herself into one giant ice cube shoveling snow from the roof.

Rory didn't object to calling it a night, though he did insist they leave the game board up so they could continue to play in the morning—no doubt because he was winning.

While he was outside bringing in a load of wood, she took the opportunity to slip into the bathroom. There was a beautiful claw-foot tub, without running water, and a chemical toilet. At this point she was grateful she didn't have to take a walk outside, and elected to wash her face with the remaining luke-warm water on the kitchen stove.

She'd managed to shed her outer clothing and slip under the covers in her longjohns by the time Rory returned.

She heard him rummaging around the potbellied stove stacking the wood.

"You okay in there?" he asked.

"Peachy keen." If you enjoyed sheets that had been kept in a freezer for half a year.

A few minutes later, he said, "Close your eyes. I'm coming in."

Instinctively, her eyes flew open. He wouldn't come into the bedroom naked, would he? Not after he'd promised—

"Watch it. You're peeking."

"I'm not!" Well, she was but she wasn't going to admit it.

Her reward for cheating was the shadowed view of an incredibly well-built man wearing his long underwear. Every muscle stood out in relief under the tight-fitting garment. Broad shoulders. Muscular arms perfectly sculpted to hold a woman. A well-developed chest where a woman could bury her head. A neat, masculine rear that invited a woman's caress. And long, strong legs.

Closing her eyes, she rolled over and stifled her groan with the pillow. When it came to Rory Oakes, she was an absolute basket case. Her only hope was a frontal lobotomy to get rid of the affliction.

She lay very still as she heard the door to the facilities open again. She listened for Rory's footsteps leaving the room. When they didn't, she tensed. What was he doing? What was he thinking?

The bed sagged as he sat down beside her, and she felt the brush of his lips against her temple, sweet and so very tempting.

"Good night, sweetheart," he whispered, his fingertips caressing her hair back from her face. "Sleep tight."

She kept her eyes squeezed tightly closed, which did nothing to slow the thundering beat of her heart.

How on earth would she ever get to sleep? Not in this lifetime. Not unless she reached up, grabbed him around the neck and dragged him into bed with her, which was exactly where she wanted him. And then she wouldn't sleep until he'd sated all the pent-up desire she'd kept in check since their summer together.

His weight lifted from the bed, and she listened to his footfalls leaving the bedroom, knowing her sexual frustration wasn't going to be eased anytime soon.

That's exactly how she wanted it, she reminded herself.

She simply hadn't realized how difficult it would be to keep her distance from the man she'd once so desperately loved.

Despite the wind that continued to batter and rattle the windows, Kristi was acutely aware of Rory in the adjacent room. She sensed more than heard his footsteps as he went to the kitchen sink. He pumped enough water for a drink, and she imagined the cool, fresh flavor of his mouth on hers. Her taste buds longed to savor again the unique essence that was Rory.

She knew when he turned off the kerosene lantern, saw the flame's last flicker and pictured Rory standing alone in the darkness. She ached with the need to go to him, to feel his arms around her, to feel safe again.

The couch creaked as he lay down. He shifted his position once, twice, apparently finding it hard to get comfortable, and she wanted him to pillow his head on her breasts. She wanted to hold him and beg him to let her stay.

A frustrated sound crowded in her throat, threatening to escape into a wail of despair. After so many years of holding her emotions in check, the bonds of restraint weakened. She needed Rory. *Wanted* him with every taut fiber of her being.

She covered her mouth with her hand and curled her body into a tight ball. Too much was at stake, the risk was too high, to succumb to her weakness now. That she would want Rory so desperately after all these years had to be a defect in her character. A wise woman would have recovered from the upheaval of a broken heart long before now. She would have moved on with her life.

But then, when it came to Rory, Kristi had never been wise.

BEING A NOBLE INDIAN wasn't all it was cracked up to be.

Rory tried to find a comfortable position on the couch. Wasn't gonna happen. The damn thing was too short and he was too aroused, unable to stop thinking of Kristi.

The quick kiss he'd given her had been a mistake. One little taste was never going to be enough. All it did was bring back memories.

And regrets.

Why hadn't he tried to track her down after he graduated from vet school? He'd had something to offer her then. But pride had kept him silent. Since she hadn't tried to reach him, he'd been afraid to take that first step.

Fool!

Now he was going to have to find a way to get past all the barriers she raised between them. Get her to trust him again. To succeed, he would gentle Kristi like he would a high-strung colt. He'd speak softly and touch her whenever he could. Get her used to him again—to his voice, his caress, even his scent.

Flipping onto to his side, he pulled the sleeping bag up over his head against the cooling temperature in the cabin. He hoped this storm would last long enough for him to wear down Kristi's resistance until she wanted him as much as he still wanted her.

THE SOUND OF THE STORM had changed.

Kristi had no idea how long it had taken her to get to sleep or what had awakened her. But something was different.

Concentrating, she lay very still. The cabin was quiet but outside the wind continued to blow, though perhaps not as hard as it had the night before. The tiniest bit of gray light seeped through the window, barely enough for her to make out the bulky shape of the chest of drawers in the corner. Dawn or close to it. But what had awakened her?

The answer came in the form of a sharp, heart-rending howl cutting through the silence. That was quickly followed by another canine voice yapping and howling in response. The sounds were coming from nearby.

Kristi sat up in bed at the same time Rory's feet hit the floor in the other room.

"Rory?" she gasped.

"I'm here." He came to the bedroom door tugging his heavy sweater on over his head. He was still wearing his longjohn bottoms that gloved his muscular legs.

"What is that noise?"

"Wolves. Sounds like one of them is hurt."

One out of how many? she wondered as the painful cries continued. "I didn't know there were wolves around here."

"They probably came down from Canada, or

maybe from Glacier National Park.'' Hopping from one foot to the other, he tugged on his jeans.

Concerned, Kristi frowned as she watched him dress. "What are you doing?"

"I'm going to take a look, see what's wrong."

"With the wolves?" She threw her covers aside, shivering in the cold air despite her thermal underwear. "You can't go wandering around out there in the middle of a pack of howling wolves."

"It's not a pack, more like a pair, I'd guess from the sound of their howls. And I don't think they're going to attack me." He stepped into his heavy snowmobile pants.

She grabbed her own sweater to put on. "Are you crazy? Or are you just trying to be a hero?"

His lips canted into a grin. "Worried about me?"

"I'm worried about myself," she lied. "How am I going to find my way back to Grass Valley if you turn yourself into a giant-size doggy biscuit?"

He had the audacity to laugh. "I promise I'll come right back."

Bold as brass he strolled into the bedroom, captured her face between his big, broad hands, dipped his head and kissed her full on the mouth. She gasped in surprise, and her lips softened instinctively, opening for him. Shock and the heat of anticipation shot through her.

He didn't take advantage of the opportunity. "Hold that thought, sweetheart. I'll be back before you know it."

She stood rooted to the spot, her lips tingling, as he stepped into his snow boots, grabbed his knit cap from the bookcase and headed for the door. He reached for the rifle he'd propped there yesterday.

"Now, wait a minute!" she said, coming back to her senses. "You can't go out there alone." She gathered up her outdoor clothing and started to dress. That kiss had been a sneak attack, darn his hide. She wouldn't let that happen again.

"Remember how cold you got yesterday? It would be smarter if you stayed inside and built up the fire."

"Yeah, like it's smart for you to risk frostbite for a wolf?"

"If it needs my help," he said simply.

There was nothing she could say that would change his mind. Rory was too darn softhearted when it came to any injured animal. But she wasn't going to let him go alone.

"If that's the case, I'm going with you."

"I'd rather you didn't."

"You know I can be as stubborn as you, don't you?"

He looked her up and down in a lazy perusal, then nodded. "Yeah, I've noticed."

While she finished dressing, Rory added wood to the fire.

"Stay right behind me," he urged as they stepped outside into the cold, gray dawn. He cradled the rifle in his arms. The weapon looked big enough to bring down an elephant, and it had a telescopic sight.

This was one time when she wasn't going to argue with Rory. Close to a foot of snow had fallen overnight, blanketing the clearing around the cabin in pristine white, and the snow was still falling in big flakes. Icicles hung from the roof at the corners of the cabin. No footprints marred the scene, not even the tracks of a passing squirrel.

The only jarring note to the postcard-perfect scene was the continuing howl of one wolf and the responding whine of another.

Kristi shuddered. Dear heaven, the poor thing must be in misery.

To her surprise Rory plucked two pairs of snowshoes from hooks on the cabin wall. She hadn't noticed them hanging there.

"I gather Jane and Everett have experienced heavy snowfalls before," she said.

"This is Montana. Snow happens."

She slipped her boots into the snowshoes. Learning to walk in them was something else again, rather like struggling through soft sand in oversize swim fins. Rory, of course, appeared not to be bothered by the awkward foot apparel.

Kristi was breathing hard by the time they'd walked a few hundred feet into the nearby stand of fir trees.

A low, threatening growl brought her to a halt.

No more than twenty feet ahead of them stood a snarling wolf, his teeth bared. Snow covered his snout, and his thick, black-and-gray coat bristled in defiance. Mounds of snow had been kicked aside all around him. The rusty teeth of a steel trap were barely visible clamped around the wolf's right-front leg.

"That's an ancient trap," Rory said in a low voice.

"No one's made them like that for fifty years or more."

"Does it belong to the Durfees?"

"Not likely. Before their time. Somebody must have had a trapline out this way and forgot where he'd placed this one." He edged sideways to get a better look. There were streaks of blood mixed with the snow around the wolf. "Looks like the wolf got a little too curious. Or hungry."

The wolf's mouth pulled back in a threatening grimace, and he followed Rory's movement with hostile golden eyes.

Beyond the trapped wolf, a lighter gray shadow moved among the trees and growled.

"Rory! There's the other one." Kristi whirled around looking for more wolves lurking nearby.

"That's his mate. She's been trying to dig him out of the trap."

The whole idea of a beautiful animal snared in the metal jaws of a trap made Kristi sick to her stomach. Trapping a squirrel was bad enough but injuring a magnificent animal like a wolf seemed criminal. In fact, it probably was. Thank goodness the Durfees weren't the criminals.

"Will she be able to get the male free?" Kristi asked.

"Not likely. His leg could already be broken, anyway, in which case he won't be able to hunt and won't survive. And if the leg isn't broken yet, he'll gnaw through it himself, just to be free."

Kristi swallowed back the bile that rose in her

throat. What desperate measures animals would take in the hope of survival.

"What can we do?" she asked.

The injured wolf gave another warning growl.

"We can take him back to the cabin and see how badly injured he is."

"Rory, I don't think that wolf is going to go with us willingly."

His smug smile was intended to goad her. "That's why I packed tranquilizer darts for the trip. You never know when they might come in handy." He reached into his inside jacket pocket, pulled out a cartridge and snapped it into the rifle, then glanced toward the trees and the second wolf. "It would help if you explained to the she-wolf that we're doing this to help her mate. If she's too possessive about this guy, she could attack us to protect him. Females can be like that."

"Nice doggy," Kristi murmured, wondering how in heaven's name she'd gotten herself into this mess.

Chapter Six

Rory eased himself into position to get a good shot at the wolf. He wasn't too worried about the female. She was wary of humans, as well she should be. But the pair were young and therefore unpredictable. That's also what had gotten the male into trouble with the trap. A more mature wolf would have known to stay clear.

He adjusted the carbon-dioxide-control valve so he wouldn't hurt the animal, aimed the rifle and squeezed the trigger. With almost no noise, the dart struck its target on the wolf's rump. The wolf reacted with a yelp and tried to shake off the dart. It stayed in position.

"How long will it take to knock him out?" Kristi asked.

"He'll go down in a couple of minutes. Then I'll carry him back to the cabin."

"I hope he's not a light sleeper."

Rory agreed. But he'd used tranquilizer darts any number of times in order to help an injured animal. This wolf shouldn't pose any particular problem.

Slowly the wolf's eyes began to glaze, and his rear end wobbled. He whined, puzzled by his inability to control his body, then sank onto the snow.

The she-wolf yipped, and danced back and forth at a safe distance, trying to encourage her mate to get up and get going. The poor guy tried but couldn't make it.

When Rory was confident the wolf was down, he walked forward, prodded the animal to make sure he was safe, then knelt beside the wolf.

"Be careful," Kristi urged.

"Keep your eye on his girlfriend, just in case."

Setting his rifle aside, he closed the wolf's eyes to protect them from the cold, dry air, then he dug down through the snow to the trap. He recoiled at the sight of the cruel instrument. He'd never been much of a hunter. He believed an animal should only be killed if it was needed for food, and then, like his Indian forebears, he gave thanks for the creature who had given its life to feed him.

Kneeling in the deep snow made his position awkward and leverage difficult to come by, but he finally released the wolf's leg from the trap. As carefully as possible he lifted the animal in his arms.

"The she-wolf behaving herself?" he asked.

"She looks worried but she's not making any moves toward you."

"Good. Get the rifle, will you?"

Kristi scrambled through the snow and picked up the rifle. "You don't really expect me to use this, do you?"

"Nope. It's not loaded."

"Great. I'll use it as a club if she attacks us."

He smiled to himself. Kristi might not be used to the outdoors but she knew how to keep her head about her and her sense of humor intact. That would be worth a lot in a medical emergency. He suspected she could handle most anything thrown her way.

Carrying a hundred pounds of deadweight wearing snowshoes made the trip back to the cabin difficult. Kristi hurried to open the door for Rory.

"The kitchen table," she said in a competent, take-charge manner. "I spotted some linens in the bedroom cupboard we can use for a clean zone. They aren't sterilized but they'll have to do."

"Perfect."

Without wasting a step, she tossed aside her mittens and hat, went to the bedroom and was back in under a minute, spreading a couple of sheets across the table.

"How much time do we have before he wakes up?" she asked.

Rory laid the wolf down. "Probably two hours, something like that."

"It took us just over fifteen minutes to walk back here. What are you going to need?" Without waiting for instructions, she began stoking the fire in the cooking stove and placed a teakettle of water on to heat.

He leaned over to examine the wolf's injury. There were several major lacerations from the trap and some bleeding and tearing from the animal's effort to escape. "I don't think any bones are broken. Of course, I can't be sure without an X ray." He glanced over his shoulder where he'd stacked their emergency gear yesterday. "There's antiseptic, sutures and antibiotics in that silver medical box. He'll need a tetanus shot, too."

Expertly, she sterilized scissors, needles and a scalpel with alcohol and laid them out with gauze and tape on a clean tray.

"You're good," he said as he began to clean the wound. "If you're ever looking for a job as a veterinarian's assistant, let me know."

"Depends on what you pay. I make pretty good money at the clinic where I'm working now."

"I probably couldn't afford to pay you much, but I'd be willing to offer some special fringe benefits."

She choked and coughed. "I'll talk to my union rep."

Chuckling, he worked on the wolf, cutting away the fur so he could see the lacerations more clearly. The trap's teeth had dug deeply into the foreleg. In one spot, clear to the bone. He rinsed the wound with a saline solution.

Meanwhile the part of his brain that was more male than veterinarian registered Kristi's fresh, outdoor scent, a mixture of snow with a hint of pine. He noted the feminine shape of her fingers, the gentle yet competent way she had about her. He imagined having her working by his side day after day, year after year.

That's not what she'd set out to do in life, he reminded himself. But she was good at rendering medical aid—on animals as well as humans. A natural. And he couldn't imagine any better way he'd like to spend his days—and his nights—than having Kristi beside him.

When he'd sutured, administered an antibiotic and wrapped the wound, Rory stretched and rotated his neck. "That's the best I can do without an X ray."

"Are you going to put him out in the snow again?"

"No. I want to observe him overnight, see how that leg is doing by morning."

"Do you plan to have him share your bed…or mine?"

"Trust me, sweetheart, I wouldn't let any other guy hop into bed with you if I could help it."

She glanced away, but not before he saw a blush rise to her cheeks.

Rory didn't want to ask too many questions about how many other men she might have known since the summer they'd spent together. That wasn't a topic he wanted to pursue. Not now. Not ever.

"I'll lock him in the shed for tonight. There's a pen the Durfees must have used for their dog. In the morning I'll see how he's doing. If he's walking okay, I'll let him go back to his ladylove."

"And if he's not?"

"I've got the feeling that if the leg isn't broken it's badly sprained. There's already some swelling. In order to recover properly, he needs to be restrained and confined for a week or more."

"I don't think either he or his girlfriend are going to like that."

"Probably not." He went to the kitchen sink to wash his hands. "They'd both like it a lot less if he was permanently disabled and not able to hunt. But that's the problem working with animals. They can't tell you what's hurting them, and you can't explain what you're doing is for the best.''

Drying his hands on a kitchen towel, he walked back to the table and stood beside Kristi, who was stroking the sleeping wolf, running her fingers through his fur.

''He's really a magnificent animal, isn't he?'' she said.

''Beautiful.'' He whispered the word, thinking of Kristi, not the animal she petted. Her hair was in disarray from wearing her cap, the strands of red and gold like tiny licks of fire, arousing his libido. Her cheeks were flushed, her lips slightly parted. Tempting.

In an imitation of her gesture, Rory laid his hand on the nape of Kristi's neck, his fingers kneading her soft flesh. Gradually the tension eased from her muscles. An audible sigh escaped her lips.

Cupping her chin, he lifted her head. Her brows pulled together above eyes dark blue with both arousal and concern.

''Rory?'' The word seemed plea and protest in the same breath.

''Nothing will happen you don't want to happen.'' As he slowly lowered his head, he waited for her to stop him. Held his breath for fear she would. Prayed he'd find the strength to stop if that was what she wanted.

At the first brush of their lips, she uttered a soft

moan. Of approval? Or refusal? Or a desire that matched his own?

The contact had been so brief, so inciting, he couldn't *not* repeat the effort. He had to be sure of her reaction. If he stopped when she didn't want him to, they would both lose the chance to pursue the passion they had once shared.

He angled her head for better access and kissed her again. This time he lingered, relishing the warmth of her lips as he nibbled lightly. Then, in turn, he suckled both top and bottom. Only his hand on her face and their lips touched. She could move away from him whenever she wanted. But she stayed, and he ventured further, letting his tongue leisurely explore the taste and texture he recalled so clearly.

Her bottom lip was lush; the upper dipped in the center in an alluring bow. Both tasted of freshly fallen snow and the subtle flavor of feminine arousal.

His body clenched, and he groaned, barely able to maintain his restraint. "I want you."

Her eyes glittered with what looked like tears when she looked up at him. Her breasts rose and fell as she took quick little breaths. "I can't—I can't do this, Rory."

It was like a winter avalanche had caught him unaware. The icy weight pressed around him, burying his hopes. He couldn't breathe. Only a well-ingrained sense of self-preservation allowed him to struggle to the surface. He filled his lungs, but the pain was more intense than he had ever expected.

"Guess I'd better take our friend out to the shed before he decides to wake up."

With a heavy heart and limbs that felt weak from lack of oxygen, he put on his snow gear and lifted the wolf from the table.

He couldn't bring himself to apologize to Kristi. He'd been honest about wanting her. He still did. That would always be with him.

KRISTI SHIVERED from the cold blast of air that swept into the cabin when Rory left, and she covered her mouth with her hand, as though that simple gesture might allow her to retain the feel of his lips on hers.

The amount of sexual chemistry in Rory's kiss was enough to set off a chain reaction. Her lips were still sizzling, and her whole body was on fire. How could she have forgotten how potent he was?

Or have underestimated how difficult it would be to resist him?

I want you had been her mantra, too.

It had taken all of her willpower not to respond more fully to Rory's kiss. She'd fisted her hand in the wolf's fur instead of threading her fingers through Rory's hair, as she had wanted to. She hadn't thrown herself into his arms, despite the desperate temptation to do so. She hadn't kissed him back, although that was exactly what her heart had cried out for her to do.

Like a flashing red light at a railroad crossing, *guilt* had stopped her from such reckless behavior.

She hadn't yet told him about his son. *Their* son.

How could she allow her passions to sweep her away when she'd kept such a shocking secret from him? It wouldn't be fair to him—or to her.

The tears that had been threatening welled up in her eyes. She swiped them away with the back of her hand. She had no idea how Rory would react to the news of his son. Until she did, she had to remain wary.

Determined to regain her self-control, she set aside the tray of medical supplies and wadded up the sheets she'd used to cover the table. She'd keep her mind occupied by keeping her hands busy. She wouldn't dwell on Rory—the past or the future.

She wouldn't think about the words she'd soon have to say that would alter her life in one way or another and the life of her son. Words she *would* have to say. He had a right to know.

But not today. Later would do.

It seemed a long time before Rory returned to the cabin. By then she'd cleaned up the evidence of the medical procedure and had started breakfast. She didn't turn to greet him.

"The best I could find for breakfast was old-fashioned oatmeal." Lifting the lid on the pot, she stirred the gruel with a big metal spoon. Adam loved oatmeal, assuming he could pile on as much sugar as he liked. "Hope that's okay."

"Have we got any sugar?"

Her hand froze in midmotion, and her heart skipped a beat. She closed her eyes. Could something so simple be genetic? "I put the sugar bowl on the table."

"Great." A chair scraped across the floor as he sat down at the table.

She scooped oatmeal into two bowls. "The wolf all right?"

"He was a little groggy when he woke up and not exactly pleased to be penned in."

Avoiding Rory's gaze, she carried the bowls to the table and returned to the counter to pour them each a mug of coffee. "How was his leg?"

"He wasn't putting any weight on it."

"He's going to be harder to examine now that he's awake." She sat down opposite Rory and watched as he sprinkled two large spoonfuls of sugar over his cereal. It was much easier to discuss the injured wolf than the kiss they had shared. Apparently Rory agreed.

"I'm going to make some kind of a muzzle I can loop over his snout. I'm not anxious for him to take a piece out of me. I may need your help to snare him."

"Of course."

He spooned some oatmeal into his mouth, tasted it and smiled. "This is good. I usually just have cold cereal and toast in the mornings."

"Oatmeal isn't that hard to make."

"Yeah, I know. But eating alone isn't all that much fun no matter what you're eating."

She didn't comment. She had breakfast with her son almost every morning. And, of course, her mother was there, too. More often than not it was Dottie Kerrigan who cooked the meals and cared for Adam while Kristi worked. Indeed, Dottie had thrived since Adam's birth, almost as though her maternal instincts had been reawakened with the arrival of a grandchild. In some ways, having a baby in the house had been both Kristi's and Dottie's salvation when Kristi's father died four years ago. Babies don't leave much time for grief.

WHEN BREAKFAST WAS OVER, Rory checked on the wolf again. He found a bag of dog food in the shed and poured some into a dish, slipping it into the pen along with a bowl of water. The wolf, his ears laid back, his yellow eyes intensely focused on Rory, was too wary to approach either dish while he was around.

"You'll want to eat later, fellow." Although the water would most likely tempt him first.

What would tempt Kristi? Rory wondered.

Despite her refusal, he sensed she'd wanted to continue their kiss earlier. Something was holding her back. But what? She'd claimed she didn't have a boyfriend, no one waiting for her at home.

He'd seen the desire in her eyes and the hint of longing. Even so, when push came to shove, she'd told him no.

Damn!

With a frustrated sigh, he powered up the generator and went back inside. The snow was still falling, though more lightly now than the previous day, and the wind had subsided. If he was going to make any headway with Kristi, time was growing short. It wouldn't be long before they had to head back to Grass Valley.

He'd never hoped for a blizzard to continue, but

that's exactly what he was thinking when he switched on the radio and called his brother.

"Can you see over the top of the snow?" he asked when Eric responded.

"Barely. We've got three families in the church shelter now, but it looks like we've seen the worst of the storm. We're hoping for some clearing tomorrow."

Rory had been afraid of that. "Then I guess we'll wait till tomorrow to come back to town."

"That would be my advice. How's it going up there?"

"Great. The cabin's real snug." Although not as cozy as Rory might have liked, wishing Kristi had been willing to snuggle with him. "I even got to play veterinarian. A young male wolf managed to step in a trap and injure himself. I tranquilized him and brought him inside, put in a few sutures. Now I've got him under observation in the shed in back of the cabin."

There was a long pause before Eric responded. "I don't know about you, Bird Brain," he drawled. "Maybe all that cold is getting to you."

"What makes you say that?"

"Seems to me if I was stranded in a remote cabin with a beautiful woman like Kristi, I'd figure out something more interesting to do with my time besides stitch up an injured wolf."

Rory grimaced. For the first time in memory, his brother was dead-on right. Unfortunately, Kristi didn't seem to agree.

He glanced in her direction. She was making a

point of studying Jane Durfee's knitting project, acting as though she hadn't heard Eric's comment. Rory might have believed her act if her cheeks weren't flushed a bright red. She'd heard, all right.

"I'll take that under advisement," he said into the mike. And hope she will, too, he mentally added.

WITHIN HOURS Kristi had gained a new understanding of the expression *cabin fever*.

It had taken her no time at all to go bankrupt when she and Rory had resumed their game of Monopoly. After that she'd tried to read but had been unable to concentrate. She'd been desperate enough for a distraction that she considered scrubbing the floor, but decided that was taking her restless feelings too far.

So she was left with only her thoughts, all of which were about Rory. His kiss. His subtle masculine scent seemed to hover in the cabin, luring her across the room to where he fiddled with the radio dials. How her body craved his touch. She longed to feel him buried deeply inside her, filling her.

For years she'd put the memory of Rory and their summer together in a secret box near her heart—not forgotten but rarely opened. Those recollections, and the disastrous ending, had been too painful to examine often. Now it was as though the lid had been ripped off the box and she couldn't snap it back into place. The images, the tactile sensations, flashed through her mind like a looping videotape in all their glorious erotic detail. In response, moisture drenched her body. She was melting from the inside out.

She hopped up from the couch. "I think I'll take a walk."

Rory glanced outside and then at her. "It's still snowing."

"We came up here in a blizzard. I don't think a little snow is going to hurt me at this point." She reached for her heavy jacket hanging beside the door. The wind had subsided to almost nothing, and the only sound was the hum of the generator that kept the radio working.

"Okay. I'll go with you."

She gritted her teeth. She needed to be away from Rory, away from the memories and the temptation he represented in the here and now. "I don't plan to go far."

"No problem. A little fresh air will do us both good." He switched off the radio.

Other than locking him in the cabin, she didn't know how she could refuse Rory's company. He had to be going stir-crazy, too, stuck inside all day. He was a virile man—too virile—and not used to being sedentary.

She stepped outside and drew a deep breath. The chill air filled her lungs and tingled her cheeks. But the moment Rory joined her on the porch she realized no matter how large a drop in temperature outside, the sensual heat that had been building within her wasn't going to cool off anytime soon.

"I'll go turn off the generator. I don't want to waste gasoline. Don't go away." He stepped off the porch into thigh-deep snow and followed his own footprints toward the back of the cabin.

Deciding a little physical exertion might cure her fixation on steamy thoughts, she grabbed a shovel they'd left on the porch and started digging a path through the snow. Moments later, her efforts focused on her work, something whapped her on her rear end.

"Hey!" She looked up just as a second snowball came hurling toward her. She tried to scramble out of the way but it caught her on the shoulder. "No fair! I wasn't ready."

Looking smug, Rory stood by the corner of the cabin. "You know what they say about love and war."

"Refresh my memory." She mashed some snow into a ball for a counterattack and let it fly.

He ducked. "That it's a great excuse for a snowball fight."

"Funny, that's not how I heard the story." She backed up a few steps to the edge of the porch, under the overhang.

"What's your version?"

"That all's fair in a snowball fight." With the shovel she whacked the side of the roof. For a moment she thought she had misjudged the depth of the snow and its weight. Then slowly the lip of snow edged forward. She was ready to dodge another missile from Rory just as the snow above him let loose. She squinted her eyes closed as he was buried beneath the unexpected avalanche.

He came up sputtering and covered from head to toe with snow. "Now, that's a declaration of war if I ever saw one." A dark, dangerous glint appeared in his eyes.

"Rory, you wouldn't take advantage of a helpless woman, would you?" she cajoled.

"Helpless, my foot." He stalked toward her.

She giggled.

He lunged at her, and she raced in the opposite direction. She could have run inside, she supposed, but what would be the fun in that?

But her pace was slowed by the deep snow. Rory was bigger and stronger. Before she had a chance to reach the relative safety of the trees, he dived for her legs and brought her down like a calf in a roping contest.

"Rory!" Breathless and laughing, she splatted facedown in the soft snow.

He rolled her over, and she looked up. His face was haloed by gently falling snowflakes, but there was nothing gentle in his eyes. They were heated and filled with sensual promise.

"Did I ever tell you about the time my brothers and I held off the entire student body of Grass Valley Unified High School during a snowball fight?" His body pressed her more deeply into the snow, and he held her hands locked together above her head. She was truly helpless—and feeling reckless.

"I don't recall that story, no." Though she could certainly believe it of the Oakes boys. All three of them had a wild side, and as teenagers they must have been the very devil to control. Oliver Oakes had done a wonderful job of taming them—or mostly so. Right now Rory resembled a wild animal on the prowl, his dark hair in disarray, his eyes glittering like polished black agates. Kristi suspected she was his prey. In her heart of hearts, she thrilled at the prospect.

"The battle lasted the entire lunch period. We'd made ourselves a fort during the morning break by piling up blocks of snow, and we'd gathered enough ammunition to fight off an army."

"So you were victorious?"

"Well, no," he conceded with a wicked grin. "Somebody called in the reserves against us."

She lifted her brows. "Reserves?"

"The vice principal. He was like a probation officer, tough as nails."

"With no sense of humor."

"You got it. Our dad wasn't pleased, either, when we were all suspended for three days. He worked our butts off around the ranch." Rory adjusted his position, lifting his weight slightly and straddling her hips. "We were still the school heroes though."

"I'm sure you were." In so many ways he'd been her hero, too. If she were honest with herself, she still thought of him that way. Except he'd hurt her so badly.

Right now their relative positions were just this side of intimate, and she could see in his eyes what it was costing him to not press the issue. To not lower his body along the length of hers, to kiss her and demonstrate the evidence of how much he wanted her. Only an honorable man would do that.

"Kristi, honey, if things have changed between us, I understand. We were kids. We've probably both changed. A lot of years have passed since—"

"No, that's not the problem. It's—there's something I have to tell you.'' Fear clogged the words in her throat that she needed to say, and she had trouble speaking.

With his gloved hand he caressed her cheek. ''Does that mean you do still want me?''

Seeking his warmth, she leaned her face into his palm. ''You know I do.''

''Then nothing you can say will stop me from wanting you.''

Chapter Seven

Her admission that she still wanted him was all the permission Rory needed. For almost six years he'd been dreaming of this moment.

He kissed her as he had earlier, but this time she gave his tongue access to explore the soft dampness of her mouth. He steeled himself not to rush. He built the anticipation, for both of them. Slowly, he tangled their tongues together, knowing later he'd revisit even more intimate places in the same way. He kissed her long and deep and endlessly.

The chill winter air in the clearing turned as warm as summer as he thought of where else he would kiss her, stroke her as he was stroking her now. He hungered for her, and felt her straining toward him, responding to her own desire.

He slid his knee between her thighs. She moved against him, uttering quiet moans of pleasure and need that brought a renewed tightness to his own body.

She hooked her arms around his neck, locking them together and lifted her hips. Even through the double thickness of their snow pants, he felt her heat against the hard ridge of his arousal.

Tossing his gloves aside, he worked his hand under her jacket. Not satisfied by the coarse feel of her wool sweater, he searched farther until he found the warmth of her flesh. Her midriff was as smooth as satin and fiery hot to his touch. He cupped the swell of her breast, kneading her with his fingers.

"Rory," she groaned, writhing beneath him. "Oh, please."

"Whatever you want, sweetheart."

"We can't—not out here."

He groaned deep in his throat, half in frustration, half in need. If it had been summer, the day sunny, the grass in the clearing warm and inviting, Rory would have loved her right there in this private glade. But he wanted to see her naked, all of her. Wanted to see what changes time had made in her. And he couldn't do that in a field covered with snow.

Shifting onto his haunches, he brought her to a sitting position. Her face was flushed, her breathing as ragged as his own.

"Inside," he whispered hoarsely.

"Yes. Please." Kristi allowed Rory to help her up, her muscles too weak and trembling to make it on her own. Never had she been kissed so thoroughly or with such erotic intensity.

The lightly falling snow muffled every sound except their heavy breathing and the crunch of their boots as they walked back to the cabin. Rory's arm was looped behind her, urging her forward. Foolish or not, fair or not, she went willingly.

Maybe now was the only chance she'd have to love him as she'd longed to do. Isolated from the world by distance and the storm, they had created their own time and space. A world apart where she could allow herself to forget the past and ignore the future. Briefly. She allayed her conscience in some small measure by knowing she had *tried* to tell him about his son.

Later she'd try again. When they returned to Grass Valley. For now she wanted to steal a few hours out of time. She'd face the consequences later.

They reached the porch, and he swung her around in front of him. "I've been too long without kissing you," he said before he lowered his head to hers again, a fierce tenderness in his eyes.

Had he always been this good at kissing? Or had it been so long since she'd been properly kissed that she was drowning in the sensations that flooded her body?

Driven by a desperate need to get closer, she unzipped his jacket and splayed her fingers across his chest. Beneath his sweater, his muscles flexed. He drew her to him. The scent of snow was all around them, mixing with the musky heat of burgeoning sex. The combination made them as wild as the landscape, as savage as two animals engaging in a primitive mating dance.

Rory unlatched the door. Almost before they were inside, they both began to shed their clothes. Jackets. Boots. Pants. Sweaters. Everything dropped to the living room floor like oversize snowflakes raining down from the sky.

The room was still warm, though the potbellied stove produced less heat than the sensual flames that licked through and around her.

He snared her with his hands around her midriff. Slowly he lifted her longjohn top until he bared her bra. With a quick flick of his fingers, he released the clasp. Finally, after what seemed a lifetime of longing for his caress, his broad palms covered her bare breasts.

She drew in a quick breath. "That feels so good," she murmured.

"To me, too."

His hands circled, his fingers kneading, his thumbs rode back and forth over the nipples, making them taut and aching for more. She made little crying sounds of pleasure. At last he dipped his head. The moist heat of his tongue replaced his hand. Kristi nearly came apart right then.

Time stood still as they urgently finished undressing each other. They shared kisses. Stroked and caressed. Rediscovered intimate secrets and erotic zones sensitive to a lover's touch. By mutual consent they sank together onto the couch, unwilling to waste the time or energy it would take to reach the bedroom, only steps away.

The sound of Rory's harsh breathing aroused Kristi beyond all measure. And then he took her higher as he slowly pushed one long finger, then two, into her intimate heat.

"Rory!" she cried aloud. Her body rocked hard and fast from the impact of her release. She'd never expected anything so explosive. Yet she should have.

She'd been storing all that energy for years waiting for Rory to free her with his potent masculine power.

He looked down at her with a combination of unabashed pleasure and unsated hunger. "Hold that thought, sweetheart. There's something I need to get out of my wallet."

She couldn't have moved if her life depended upon it. "You brought condoms?" She was pleased with his foresight but a little miffed he'd been so sure of himself.

He eased off the couch onto his feet and stood there, naked and magnificent, his skin burnished by the sun and his Indian ancestry. "The moment I discovered you were back in town, I started wanting you. Call it blind hope, if you'd like, but I figured if there was a chance I'd better be prepared."

Moments later he returned and sat down beside her. Shamelessly, she reached for the silver packet in his hand. Even though Kristi, of all people, knew condoms didn't offer one-hundred percent protection, she was willing to take the gamble again.

"Let me do it," she whispered. With shaking hands, she opened the packet and slowly sheathed his erection.

He settled between her legs. His hands soothed down the sides of her thighs and he lifted her hips. "I've missed you so much."

She sobbed with joy as he thrust into her. He waited a moment for her to adjust to his penetration and then he began a slow rhythmic rocking. Impossibly, her body responded as though she hadn't only minutes ago experienced an earthshaking climax.

She closed around him. Arching her back, she raised her legs to allow him even deeper access. The pressure increased. The friction sent waves of hedonistic pleasure through her.

"Rory, I can't—"

"Stay with me, Sparkles. This is the real deal."

She held on for all she was worth, thrilled at his use of her nickname, a reminder of a fireworks celebration at a rodeo they'd enjoyed together. She watched him watching her, remembering how he'd told her she was more incandescent than sky rockets. Heat blazed in his dark eyes and sped through her bloodstream. She trembled on the brink of a new climax and then she was swept past the abyss. With another thrust, Rory joined her and there was no turning back.

For a long while, Kristi drifted in an ethereal state of pleasure. Rory's weight pressed down on her. The cushions on the couch were lumpy with little room to move. Even so she felt as though she were floating on a cloud.

Gradually, the air in the cabin cooled. The fire in the potbellied stove needed to be stoked, but Kristi was in no hurry. She hadn't felt this content for years. Or more cherished.

"I'm going to have to get up," Rory murmured, his warm breath teasing over her right ear. "I must be squashing you."

"Don't leave on my account. I like you right where you are." If she had her way, he'd always be within her embrace. Which might make it a little difficult to do her work at the clinic, she thought, a tiny giggle erupting.

"This isn't a laughing matter, Sparkles. I'm not sure I have the strength to budge. You don't have any idea what your laughing does to me."

Actually, she did. They were still linked together, and she felt his reaction intimately.

"I don't know how you managed to sleep on this couch last night" she said. "It's way too short for you."

"I'm thinking of giving the bed a try tonight."

She brushed a kiss to his cheek and stroked her hand down the smooth plains and valleys of his back. "I think that's a really good idea."

In the distance, a wolf howled a mournful sound, which was answered with a plea from the wolf penned in the shed out back. With the light fading in the cabin and night coming on, the sound could not have been more lonely. Kristi shivered at the memory of how many years she'd felt just as alone.

Rory eased his weight away from Kristi, shifting his position to sit on the edge of the couch. Idly, he stroked her breast, sending frissons of renewed pleasure through her.

"Sounds like our guy's girlfriend is lonely and plans to stick around," Rory said.

"Females spend a lot of their time waiting for a guy."

"Do they?"

Years ago she'd waited too long, lunging for the phone whenever it rang, desperate for his call. His silence had been like a barbed arrow through her heart. The wound still hadn't entirely healed.

Suddenly aware of her nakedness, she scooted around to sit up. Clothes littered the floor, his and hers all mixed together.

How could he have found another woman so quickly? She'd been devastated by the realization then, and still hadn't quite accepted that it was true. But the truth was, nearly six years had passed, and he had never once tried to contact her. That should tell her something.

His incredible lovemaking told her something else.

The net result was confusion mixed with a whole lot of residual pain.

Rory gathered up his clothes and began putting them on. "I'd better check on my patient. Then we can do dinner."

"You mean you're hungry for food again?"

He shot her a rakish grin. "I plan to use up a lot of calories this evening, and not by playing Monopoly. I might consider a game of strip poker, though, assuming you promise to lose."

In spite of herself, Kristi flushed. She hadn't planned to make love with Rory. But once he'd slipped past her barriers, she knew she was defenseless. No way could she refuse him, because that would be denying herself the pleasure she longed to experience again.

Tomorrow, when they returned to Grass Valley, would be time enough for the confrontation she knew was coming.

Tonight she'd put her conscience on hold—and the

sense of betrayal that lingered right below the surface of her awareness.

RORY HUNKERED DOWN beside the pen to observe the injured wolf. Unblinking yellow eyes filled with accusation gazed back at him. With a low snarl the wolf pulled his lips back to reveal his teeth. Outside, the female called again to her partner.

"I know you'd like to be outta here," Rory conceded, noting the wrap on the animal's leg was still intact. "But it looks to me like your leg is still swollen. You've got yourself a bad sprain." The animal had managed to eat a few bites of the dog food and drink a little water, but hadn't moved to the far corner of the pen, which would have been the natural thing to do. That led Rory to believe walking was painful for the wolf and would hamper him for some days.

The female's tormented cry floated through the cold air of the shed.

"You're some lucky dude. Your girlfriend seems determined to stick around. At least for now."

Rory wondered what would induce Kristi to stay in Grass Valley longer than she had planned. Or if she would even consider the possibility. If she based her decision on how great they were together in bed, he'd have a good shot at getting her to stay. They'd pretty well set the cabin on fire, they were so darn hot together. Even better than when they'd both been young and mostly inexperienced.

Sparkles. His own personal sky rocket.

He grinned at the memory of this afternoon. Man, she was one sexy lady who gave as good as she got.

Her uninhibited response had nearly sent him over the edge before they got started. It had been all he could do to control himself until they were inside the cabin where they wouldn't freeze their buns off—literally.

The snow had almost stopped falling by the time he headed back inside. As the temperature dipped, it turned the snow on the ground to crystals that caught in the faint twilight and sparkled like tiny diamonds. A few stars had begun to show in the darkening sky.

The wolf in the shed and his mate were too young to have produced a litter yet. So far they'd just been playing house. Next season the female would be holed up in a den, puppies suckling at her teats. The beginning of a new wolf pack.

In some ways during the summer he'd shared with Kristi, they'd both been playing house, not mature enough to make the commitment necessary to hold a relationship together for the long haul. He was older and more settled now. Kristi was, too.

He stepped onto the porch, stomped the snow from his boots. A rush of tenderness swept through him as he pictured Kristi nursing the baby they could create together. Maybe his brother Walker wasn't the only one lucky enough to have a family of his own.

A racket from inside the cabin jerked him back to reality, and he shoved open the door. Kristi was standing in the middle of the room, dressed in her flannel shirt and oversize jeans, swaying to the world's most scratchiest music. *If* you could call it music at all.

"What's going on?" he asked.

"Isn't it great?" Grinning, she stepped aside to show him an ancient hand-cranked Victrola with a huge brass horn. "We get to have music with our dinner."

"Sounds like a surefire route to indigestion to me." He examined the leather-covered wooden box and the turntable inside with a 78-rpm record circling beneath a mechanical arm. No stereo here, barely mono, and the tinny timbre of the music plus the occasional pop were enough to set his teeth on edge.

"It looks like the Durfees have a serious collection of old cowboy music," she said.

"You mean country-western?" Rory didn't recognize the song that was playing, and he'd been known to spend a spare evening or so doing some fancy two-stepping at the local saloon.

"Nothing so modern." She opened the cabinet beneath the Victrola where records were neatly stacked on edge in a metal rack. "We're talking Sons of the Pioneers, Riders of the Purple Sage, a dozen or more Gene Autry records."

"Sounds like the Durfees have either been hermits too long, or they both have gone deaf."

"Oh, you!" Laughing, she punched him lightly on his biceps. "Don't be such a stick-in-the-mud. These are absolute classics."

"If you say so." He loved the sparkle in her eyes, the flushed excitement in her cheeks. If all it took was an old Victrola to make her happy, he'd buy a dozen of them. "Personally, I'd rather hear something we could dance to."

"Dance? I think we can arrange that." Kneeling, she searched through the record collection.

The needle reached the end of the record on the turntable and scooted to the center. Rory lifted the arm and put it in its holder.

"We could turn on the generator and listen to a broadcast station on the radio," he suggested.

"What would be the challenge in that?" she countered as she switched the first record for another one. "Your turn to crank."

Shaking his head in amusement, he did as she asked. She released the brake, the record began to turn, and she lowered the needle into place. The sound of the song "Tumbling Tumbleweed" filled the cabin, scratchy but the words sung by the male chorus understandable.

"Come on, hotshot. Show me your stuff." She stepped toward him.

He shrugged out of his jacket and tossed it in the general direction of the couch. "Fair warning. I'm likely to step on your feet with my boots, and you don't have any shoes on."

"I'll risk it."

Rory saw no reason to argue further. He pulled her close and slid both arms beneath her shirt, splaying his fingers across her back. He didn't plan any fancy footwork. Swaying with her in rhythm to the old song was good enough for him. He especially liked the way her breasts pressed against his chest, the curve of her back beneath his hand and her own special scent as she rested her head against his shoulder. In unison, they moved in slow, sensual steps.

"Now, don't you agree this is more romantic than two-stepping?" she murmured.

"Hmm." He nuzzled her hair. "Doing anything with you is fine by me." Except, now his body was beginning to react to their slow dance, wanting more. He angled his head for a kiss and he found her warm, inviting lips.

The record ended, the needle screeching as it slid out of the groove. Rory ignored it. So did Kristi.

"Let's try the bed this time," he said when he came up for air.

"You don't want to foxtrot to 'Happy Trails'?" she asked innocently. "I saw the record in the—"

With a low growl that was half laughter, he kissed her into silence, making his preference clear.

MORNING BROUGHT a pale-blue sky, warming temperatures and a mild sense of anxiety to Kristi. With the passing of the storm, she and Rory were no longer snowbound. Their passionate interlude, which had brought Kristi such pleasure, was about to end. They'd be returning to Grass Valley this morning— and reality.

As she finished up their breakfast dishes and put them away, Rory was talking with his brother on the radio.

"The plow made it to town last night," Eric reported. "An ambulance followed it the whole way, and they hauled Everett off to Great Falls to the hospital. The latest report has him in stable condition."

Rory glanced in Kristi's direction and smiled. "We're both glad to hear Everett's doing okay."

"Everything is mostly back to normal here," Eric said, "although I expect we'll get some tourists dropping by pretty soon. Grass Valley made the big-time TV news."

"How come?"

"Because we were cut off from the outside world, according to the newscasters, who don't realize this happens almost every winter. A couple of days without the outside world impinging on our sublime community isn't that big a deal."

Rory chuckled. "As soon as we get things tidied up here, we'll be heading back."

"Don't rush on our account. Things are under control. I can tell everybody it's still snowing where you are. You two can take your time, enjoy yourselves."

Rory's gaze met Kristi's, questioning her. She was tempted. What would a day or two hurt? Still, she'd come to Montana to help her grandmother. It seemed irresponsible to linger in an isolated cabin indulging herself in mind-blowing sex when her grandmother couldn't even climb the stairs in her own house.

More than that, she had to tell Rory about Adam and didn't want to do that until she was on safe ground.

"We'd better go back." Her throat filled with regret that their special time together was ending, and her voice was hoarse with trepidation about what might come next.

Rory keyed the mike, but his eyes never left hers. "We'll be back by early afternoon."

THE RETURN TRIP was much easier than the initial journey. The warming sun danced off the snow, making Kristi squint despite her tinted helmet visor.

Rory had transformed a wooden crate from the Durfees' shed into a cage. Getting the injured wolf into the box and the box strapped onto the sled behind his snowmobile was somewhat more complicated. With the help of the muzzle snare he'd devised and a little prodding from Kristi, the wolf finally hobbled into the box. Kristi could only imagine how distressed his mate must be when she caught a glimpse of the female lurking in the trees not far from the shed. But she agreed the male would never survive if released before he was well enough to hunt.

She straddled the snowmobile and started the engine. "Will the wolf's mate wait for him to come back?" she asked Rory as they got underway.

"She may," he responded via the helmet radio. "They're a pretty young pair. It depends on how closely they have bonded."

Kristi had bonded with Rory almost six years ago. Her heart was still coupled with his, the link unbroken on her side of the chain. But she wasn't sure he had forged an equally strong bond in return.

She only had a few days left to find out—and to tell him about his son, news that could shatter whatever connection they had reestablished.

The slower pace demanded by hauling the crate on the sled meant she could more fully enjoy the pristine scenery en route, a landscape scrubbed clean by the new-fallen snow. She felt a twinge of regret as they reached the outskirts of Grass Valley, their snowmobiles skidding along the recently plowed road, and a renewed sense of unease.

Rory turned onto the side road that led to Justine's clinic and his veterinary practice.

As Kristi pulled to a stop, she noticed a familiar car in her grandmother's circular driveway. A car with Washington license plates.

She switched off the snowmobile just as the front door to Justine's home burst open. A child with dark hair, a beautiful smile and wide black eyes burst outside and came running toward her.

"Mommy! Mommy! Grandma and me came to see Grandma Justy, too!"

Belatedly, Kristi realized she'd waited too long to tell Rory the truth. Adam looked so much like his father with his dark hair and flashing dark eyes, her secret would be apparent to everyone who met the boy.

Including Rory.

Chapter Eight

Shock drove Rory from the snowmobile that he'd parked behind Kristi's machine. He wrenched off his helmet, letting it slip from nerveless fingers onto the snow in Doc Justine's driveway. Dumbstruck, he watched as Kristi knelt, and the little boy ran happily into his mother's arms.

Kristi had a son? His head reeled with the sudden revelation, and the earth seemed to tilt on its axis.

Why hadn't she mentioned the boy? They'd been stranded together in a cabin for two days, and she hadn't so much as dropped a hint. Why the hell not?

The youngster's hair was as black as raven wings, his cheeks chubby to go with his sturdy young body, his complexion shades darker than Kristi's fair skin. Although Rory wasn't much of a judge, he guessed the child's age to be about five.

A prickling sensation crept down Rory's spine, and a knot tightened in his gut. Who was the boy's father?

"We missed you, Mommy."

Kristi returned the youngster's hug, kissing the

boy. "I missed you, too, champ." She finger combed her son's dark hair back from his forehead.

"Grandma Justy said it was okay for us to come visit so we got in Grandma's car and drove and drove until Grandma told me to stop asking if we was there yet." His feet shuffled back and forth as though standing still was beyond his ability. "And then we was here."

"Yes, I can see that." Kristi stood, her arm protectively around the boy's shoulder. Her gaze met Rory's, a hint of defiance in her eyes, which didn't quite match the nervous sweep of her tongue across her lips. "Rory, I'd like you to meet my son, Adam."

Without waiting for any further introduction, the boy shrugged away from his mother and said, "Hi. My name's Adam William Kerrigan and I just turned five years old." He stomped through the trampled snow of the driveway and extended his hand to Rory. "That means pretty soon I can be in regular kindergarten. Miss Zidbeck says she'll be glad to see me gone cuz I talk too much."

A painful lump formed in Rory's throat. Slipping off his heavy snow glove, he extended his hand to the boy. He wanted to say something to the youngster, but myriad emotions tangled his tongue and squeezed his heart. The boy didn't seem to notice.

"Can I have a ride on your snowmobile?" he asked, his feet already in motion toward the vehicle. "I've got a helmet at home but I didn't bring it with me. You could give me one, though. What's in the box on the sled?"

Rory found his voice. "Stay away from the crate,

son.'' *Son.* The word slipped past his tongue on a whisper. Was it possible? Surely she would have told him. That wasn't a secret a woman had a right to keep. ''There's a wolf inside. We don't want to frighten him.''

''A real one?'' Eager eyes as dark as his own looked up at Rory.

''Adam!'' Kristi lunged toward her son, snaring him before he could investigate the contents of the crate. ''It's cold out here, and you don't have your jacket on. Let's go inside before you get chilled.'' She turned the boy toward the house.

''Can I see the wolf later, Mom? Can I?''

''We'll see, dear.''

''I bet he's got real big teeth.'' He looked up at Rory as his mother propelled him along. ''Does he gots real big teeth, mister?''

Rory nodded. ''Big enough.''

''Wow! Wait till I tell Troy. Bet he's never seen a real wolf.''

The front door of the house opened, and a middle-aged woman appeared. Her hair was a deep auburn, her physical resemblance to Kristi close enough for Rory to guess this was her mother, Dottie Kerrigan.

''Hello, dear,'' her mother called, waving. ''Hope you don't mind we came to see Grandma Justy, too.'' Slowly she slid her gaze from her daughter toward Rory, her smile uncertain.

Intent on questions of his own, he didn't acknowledge the woman.

When it looked as though Kristi might escape into the house with her son, Rory spoke her name sharply.

She turned around to face him.

"I have to kennel the wolf. After that, you and I need to talk." Rory spoke in a tone meant to leave no doubt about his intentions. "Be at my place in thirty minutes."

Slowly, she nodded. "Thirty minutes. I'll be there."

Making an about-face, Rory mounted his snowmobile and drove across the side street to his own place. How could Kristi have made love with him with such total abandon at the cabin and at the same time been deceiving him in the most heartless way? It didn't seem possible, yet the evidence was compelling.

A jumble of emotions snagged in Rory's chest.

In the kennel area, which was well away from the penned elk he'd rescued a week ago, Rory stacked bales of hay inside a pen to create a makeshift den for the wolf, all the while searching for the peace Jimmy Deer Running had taught him to seek when anger and resentment threatened to overwhelm him. The Blackfeet tribal leader had not given him enough skills to overcome the wrenching emotions that battered him from the inside out.

A son!

Without Kristi's admission of guilt, he couldn't be one-hundred percent sure, but Adam had to be his. The boy was clearly of Indian descent. It didn't take high math to add up the numbers. Rory and Kristi had been together during the summer months. The child's birthday was in the spring. That equaled nine months!

His breath caught, and he fell to his knees beneath the combined weight of guilt and fury, his anger directed both at himself and Kristi.

Why hadn't she told him?

He staggered back to the sled and shoved it to the kennel gate. Once the wolf realized he was free to leave the box, he hobbled into the wire enclosure. Standing quietly beside the box, Rory observed the wolf trying to make sense of his new world.

Taming his own twisting, twirling thoughts, grasping his new reality was even more difficult for Rory.

Finally he heard the crunch of footsteps in the snow behind him, then silence. He waited.

"I tried to tell you." Her voice barely carried to him.

His fingers clenched into fists. "When?"

"At the cabin. Before we made love."

He shot her a look over his shoulder. "He's five years old, Kristi. Was that the first time it occurred to you I'd be interested to learn I had a son?"

Her chill-reddened cheeks paled even as she lifted her chin a notch. "I tried to tell you before, too. When I was pregnant. You didn't bother to return my phone calls."

"I didn't—" He narrowed his eyes. "What phone calls? You never called me, never sent me a letter."

"I called you at school when I realized I was pregnant. A half-dozen times. I left messages. Nothing happened, Rory. I waited by the phone and it never rang. And when that woman told me not to bother you again, I got the message loud and clear. You'd found someone else."

Rory searched his memory for a woman, any woman who might have been answering his phone. A moment ago he'd thought he was the victim here, the one kept in the dark, but Kristi was acting as though she was the one who'd been betrayed. "I don't know what you're talking about. There wasn't any woman. I didn't have time for a woman. Because of my dyslexia, I had to study twice—no, three times as hard as anybody else just to stay afloat."

She folded her arms across her chest. "Studying while in the shower is certainly an odd way to drum information into your head."

"I have no idea what you're talking about."

"The last time I called, a woman answered. She told me you were in the shower and she was about to join you there. She said not to bother calling again because you and she—" Despite her bravado, Kristi's chin quivered and a sheen of tears appeared in her eyes. Angrily, she swiped them away with the back of her hand. "What was I supposed to think?"

"That you had the wrong number, for God's sake. There wasn't—" He halted in midthought. He'd hired a grad student to tutor him in biology and anatomy. Diane. Diane something. He couldn't even remember her last name. But they'd spent a lot of time together, much of it in his closet-size apartment. She'd come on to Rory a couple of times, but he hadn't taken the bait. Could she have—

"I gather I've managed to jog your memory," Kristi said.

"Yeah. There was one woman—"

Kristi visibly shuddered. "Then you can understand why I didn't think you'd appreciate my timing or the news that I had to share, since you'd so quickly and conveniently moved on with your life.''

"It wasn't like that." In three steps Rory closed the distance between them. His fingers flexed with the need to grab her—to shake some sense into her or hold her tight, he couldn't be sure which. So he fisted his hands at his side. "I hired a tutor. A woman. I was flunking out of half my classes and I had to do something."

"Taking showers together seems a little outside the typical job description for a tutor."

"I *didn't* take a shower with her. God's truth. But she could have answered the phone once or twice."

"And erased the messages on your answering machine?"

He rolled his eyes. Had Diane been that devious? Hell, he didn't know. "It's possible. I had a roommate. He was kind of flaky. He could have erased my messages. I spent a lot of time in the library because he insisted on playing his CDs at full volume." Rory had seen remarkably little of Lyle Gomez, and then he'd dropped out of school leaving Rory with half the rent unpaid.

"You have an answer for everything, don't you?"

He bristled at her accusation. "And you've got a really good reason for not having tried again to let me know about the boy in the past five years? A postcard would have been nice."

Kristi glanced around as though checking to see if anyone was listening. At midafternoon, the sun cast long shadows across the fast-melting snow, leaving rivulets of water running down the plowed street and dripping from rooftops. They should have taken their conversation inside, but apparently neither of them had the will or the desire to be alone together. Not now when their emotions were so volatile.

"What would you have done if I'd reached you, Rory? And told you I was pregnant?"

"I'd have married you in a heartbeat," he said without hesitation.

"And then?"

He wasn't quite sure what she was asking. "I guess I would have gotten a job, or come back to the ranch to work the place with Walker."

"You would have given up your dream of becoming a veterinarian?"

"I sure wouldn't have turned my back on my own kid. Or you. My mom dumped me when I wasn't much older than Adam is now. You can't think for a minute I'd—"

"I only knew you weren't there when I needed you."

Rory swore, low and succinctly. "Okay, maybe we both screwed up. What are we going to do now? Does the boy know I'm his father?"

She pursed her lips. "No. I had no idea how you would react when I told you about him, and I certainly didn't expect Adam and my mother to show up here now."

"I just bet that's the case. And if he hadn't shown up, maybe I still wouldn't know."

"I was going to tell you. That's half the reason I agreed to help Grandma Justine when she broke her ankle. It was time you knew. But I had to think of my son, too. If you'd rejected him, I wasn't going to subject him to that. He would have been better off not knowing about you.''

Rory didn't know whether to believe Kristi or not. His world had been so turned upside down, he didn't know what to believe anymore. ''I want Adam to know I'm his dad, and I want him to know I didn't know he existed until this afternoon.''

''What's he going to think of me—''

''Frankly, at this point, I don't give a damn. I would never turn my back on my own kid, and you should have known that from the get-go. If you don't want to tell him, I will.''

''I'd like a chance to prepare him—''

''You've had *five* years, Kristi. That's all the time you get.''

For a moment it looked as though she might argue with his ultimatum but then she relented with a curt nod. ''You won't take your anger at me out on my son, will you?''

''*Our* son.'' He sighed, a mixture of relief and trepidation. ''And, no, I just want him to know—''

His voice caught. This child Kristi had borne was a stranger to him, yet he wanted to be able to give the world to the boy. He wanted to be a loving father. Teach him to track deer through the woods, follow the trail of a raccoon, appreciate the flight of an eagle. He wanted to share so much with his son. And suddenly he felt totally inadequate for the job.

He fought back the tears that welled up in his eyes.

"Tell Adam he can come see the wolf. We'll start with that."

SHAKEN BY HER ENCOUNTER with Rory, Kristi walked across the road to her grandmother's home and clinic. Normally the sight of organized chaos in the entry hall and the scent of antiseptic soothed Kristi, reminding her of her roots and the gruff, unconditional love she'd experienced in her grandmother's house. Today it wasn't enough to quiet the riot of emotions pummeling her.

Rory hadn't gotten her messages? There hadn't been another woman? Had Kristi allowed a stranger to mislead her into believing a lie? Or had embarrassment and her own sense of inadequacy been at fault? She'd been so darn young and inexperienced.

But that wasn't the whole story. Whatever else had happened, Rory had never tried to contact her. The same nearly six years had passed for him as it had for her. If he'd been interested, he could have called or written. If nothing else, Grandma Justine would have contacted her if Rory had said the word.

If blame needed to be placed, it had to be shared. The only one who was innocent was Adam.

Slipping out of her jacket, she hung it on a peg near the doorway. Her mother and grandmother were both sitting in the living room drinking coffee.

"Where's Adam?" Kristi asked. For almost six years, her secret had weighed heavily on Kristi's shoulders. Now, with the time at hand to reveal the truth to her son, she felt weak from carrying the burden for so long.

"Upstairs," Justine volunteered. "He's playing computer games."

Hoping that would hold her son's interest for a little while, Kristi turned her attention to her mother. "I thought we'd discussed my leaving Adam at home so his routine wouldn't be interrupted. You know he gets hyper if there are too many changes in his life."

Dottie lifted her shoulders in a shrug of innocence. "The TV news was all about Grass Valley being isolated by the storm. I got worried about you and—"

"That's not really why you came, is it?" Kristi accused.

Setting her coffee mug on an end table, Dottie stood. She angled her chin in the same way Kristi had often seen reflected in her own mirror when her stubborn streak was aroused.

"That young man on the snowmobile is the one, isn't he?" Dottie asked.

Kristi shot a glance at her grandmother. "Did you tell her?"

"Heavens, no." Justine's leg was propped on a footstool, her bare toes covered by a gray wool sock. "I've kept my word all these years. But your mother isn't stupid. She'd have to be blind not to recognize Rory as Adam's father the moment she saw him."

"Either you or Justine should have told me," Dottie insisted. "All these years—"

"All these years are about to come to an end. Rory and I are going to tell Adam now."

"About time," Justine groused. "That's exactly what I hoped would happen when I asked you to come baby-sit me and my practice."

"You what?" Kristi gasped.

"You and that animal doctor need to clear the air between you, and the boy needs to know his own daddy. You've been putting it off for too long, child, and I'm fed up keeping your secret. Better to get it out in the open."

Mentally, Kristi backtracked. "You *begged* me to come here so I'd be forced to deal with Rory? Not because you actually needed my help at the clinic?"

"Of course I needed you. Still do." She gestured vaguely toward the clinic. "But getting you and Rory together is a heck of lot more important than giving a few folks shots in their respective rear ends."

"You had no right to bring me here under false pretenses."

"You two youngsters—you and Rory—were as sweet a couple as I'd ever seen that summer. You should have gotten married then."

Dottie shot her mother a horrified look. "I wish you'd done a better job of chaperoning Kristi. Maybe she wouldn't have—"

"It wasn't Grandma's fault," Kristi said in Justine's defense. Maybe they would have gotten married, if Kristi had been able to reach Rory and he had done the noble thing—given up his dream to become a veterinarian.

"I would have had to sit on top of those two youngsters 24/7 to keep them apart, and I wasn't about to do that," Justine insisted. "Their juices were flowing, that's what. From the way they looked at each other a couple of nights ago, I suspect they still are."

A blush heated Kristi's cheeks. Her grandmother, as usual, was far too perceptive. But she didn't appreciate Justine's interference. Or her efforts at matchmaking.

"Mom!" Adam's thundering footsteps on the stairs preceded his appearance en route to the front door. "I'm gonna build a snow fort and then I'm gonna—"

"Whoa, young man!" Her heart suddenly in her throat, Kristi snared her son before he could get out the door. "How would you like to visit Rory's wolf?"

"Wow! Can I?"

"He specifically invited you to come visit."

Kristi's mother followed her into the entryway. "Do you want me to come with you?" Dottie asked. "It's going to be hard to—"

"No." Impulsively, Kristi gave her mother a hug. "It's best if Rory and I do this together."

Tears formed in Dottie's pale-blue eyes. "I love you, honey. So did your dad. Whatever happens, that won't change."

"I know, Mom."

She picked up her son's jacket, which had fallen to the floor, and plucked her own off the wall hook. "Come on, champ. This is going to be a real treat for you. Rory Oakes knows more about wolves than anyone I know." She left unsaid the news that Rory was also her son's father—news that might shatter Adam's faith in her.

RORY SAW THEM crossing the road, and his courage faltered. What should he say? How could a man announce to a five-year-old kid that he was the boy's father? A father he'd never seen in his life and probably resented like hell because he hadn't been around.

That's how Rory had felt about his father. *That* man, his biological father, hadn't given a damn about him. Or his mother, who had been equally eager to rid herself of him before he was eight. Rory's feelings of inadequacy, of being unlovable, had haunted him all of his life. Including now.

Rory swore under his breath. Even as a kid, he'd vowed he'd never be like his dad. Or his mother.

Oliver Oakes had been different, welcoming Rory into his home, his life, with all the love he could muster. And some damn stern discipline when Rory had needed it as an adolescent. Forcefully, he tried to focus on the love and caring his adoptive father had taught him, hoping it would outweigh other lessons he had learned.

Straightening his shoulders, he walked toward his son.

"Hey, kiddo. Want to take a look at the wolf?"

"Yeah. Can I?"

"You bet." He knelt in front of the boy. Unable to help himself, he feathered the child's razor-straight hair away from his forehead with his fingers. "We have to be real quiet, though. Wild animals get spooked easy. We don't want to scare the wolf. He could hurt himself if he gets too frightened."

Adam's eyes rounded with excitement. "I can be quiet if I hafta."

"I'm sure you can, son. I'm sure you can." Emotion crowded in Rory's throat as he took the boy's hand, so small and trusting. He led him to the wolf's kennel. At some level he was aware that Kristi followed them, but for now all of his attention was on Adam—*his son.*

A few feet from the wire enclosure, Rory crouched down. Adam did the same.

"Where is he?" the boy asked, his effort at whispering loud enough to be heard in the next block. "I don't see nuthin'."

"See how the hay is stacked so there's an opening. That's the wolf's den. You can just see him inside. His fur's gray and black."

"Ooooh!" Adam edged forward. "I see him. He's got *yellow* eyes."

"Yep. And he doesn't quite know what to make of us."

"Wow! Wait till I tell Troy. Can I pet him?"

Rory restrained the boy before he got any closer to the chain-link fence. "No way, son. Wild animals don't like to be petted."

"Is that how come you put him in a cage?"

"I put him there because he hurt his leg in a trap. If I let him go now, he wouldn't be able to hunt for himself. I'll release him when his leg heals."

The youngster considered Rory's words. "Did he bite you when you caught him?"

"Nope. I tranquilized him with a dart gun."

"Cool."

"If I hadn't, the wolf would have tried to bite me. He still would if I went inside the cage with him.

That's how most animals act—even pets—when they're afraid.''

"Mom and me gots a dog."

"Really? What kind?"

"He's big and shaggy. Mom says he looks like a rug. We call him Ruff cuz he likes to bark. Mom says I hafta to feed him every, every day and never forget."

"It's good that you're learning to be responsible for your pet."

The boy hung his head. "Sometimes Mom has to remember for me."

Unable to resist, Rory hooked his arm around the child's shoulder, drawing him closer. The boy seemed so small, yet he was already halfway grown. Rory had missed seeing Adam as a newborn, he'd been denied the right to watch the boy crawl or take his first steps. He'd gone to school without Rory at his side.

Tears blurred his vision, obscuring the kennel and the wolf, leaving only a sharp understanding of what he had missed.

How could Kristi have taken all of that from him? Not given him the choice to be a father to the boy?

How had he been so absorbed in his studies to let it happen?

Coming to his feet as painfully as an arthritic old man, he said, "Come on, kiddo. I'll show you and your mom my clinic."

"Are you a doctor like my grandma Justy?"

"Nope. Doc Justine can only handle patients with two legs. My patients have four."

With his head tipped back, Adam studied Rory for a minute and then grinned. "You're an animal doctor!"

"Got it in one, champ."

With the use of Kristi's affectionate name for her son, Rory's gaze met hers. She'd waited a few feet behind them while he'd shown Adam the wolf. Now he noted tears in her eyes, and she looked pale with anxiety. He couldn't do anything about that. She'd had five years to think about this moment. He was stuck improvising.

Despite the knot in his stomach, he hooked his arm over the boy's shoulder again, urging him toward the building that housed his animal clinic. Suddenly, the thought of telling Adam that he was his father, in the cold, antiseptic environment of the clinic, felt all wrong.

"Hey, I've got a better idea. I've got the makings of hot chocolate at my house, and I could probably scrounge up some marshmallows if I look hard enough. Whadaya think?"

Adam pumped his fist in the air. "Hot chocolate!"

KRISTI TRAILED after Rory and her son like a distant, unwelcome relative. She'd seen how caring Rory was with Adam. She'd recognized the underlying pain that had made his voice more hoarse than usual. He might well prefer having time with his son alone, but she wasn't going to let him break the news of his paternity without her being present.

Adam's emotions could be volatile. His preschool teacher was convinced he had attention deficit disorder—ADD. The woman had urged he be given medication. Kristi had rejected the idea.

From her perspective, Adam was simply an active, energetic little boy, if somewhat on the hyper side. Certainly more verbal than most for his age. She also knew the downside of overmedicating children and the potential for long-term negative effects. That wasn't a risk she was willing to take with her son.

He did, however, need a firm, calm hand. Despite her own overwrought emotional state, she intended to be there when Adam learned Rory was his father.

Rory's house was a modest, one-story bungalow. He led them in the back door through a mudroom to the equally modest kitchen, which was amazingly neat for a bachelor. There were no high-tech appliances apparent, only basic equipment—a gas stove run by a propane tank she'd seen outside. A double sink with a garbage disposal. Vinyl countertops that appeared well aged, and equally vintage flooring. A small microwave that appeared to be the more used appliance in the place.

To counteract the otherwise plain surroundings, pots of lush potted vines filled a window box above the sink, and a geranium plant in full bloom sat in the center of the kitchen table.

"I'm still trying to fix things up," Rory said as they passed through the kitchen into small living room furnished with a couch, recliner and TV. Veterinary and rodeo magazines lay in disarray on a low coffee table along with a half-consumed mug of coffee. "Updating the clinic comes first."

Kristi understood his priorities. It couldn't be easy

to start a new veterinary practice. Extras for the house would come last, though she could easily imagine sprucing the place up with some cheery homemade curtains, a few inexpensive pictures on the wall, a bright rag rug in front of the cozy fireplace. It wouldn't take all that much time or money—

Abruptly, she brought her thoughts to a halt. It wasn't her job to redecorate Rory's home. She'd come here for only one reason, and that was to tell Adam that Rory was his father.

Beyond that, nothing else was important. Whatever dreams, whatever fantasies, she'd had at the cabin with Rory were moot now. She could only think about her son.

Chapter Nine

Rory made hot chocolate while Adam turned the recliner into a jungle gym and Kristi paced.

"Here we go," Rory said, returning to the living room with three mugs on a tray. "How 'bout you and your mom sit on the couch," he said to Adam. "We've got, uh, something to tell you."

He glanced at Kristi and saw the plea in her eyes, the worry that their announcement would in some way hurt the boy. Only hours ago he'd been making love to this woman, holding her, kissing her. His body clenched at the memory of her fiery response, her cries of release when he'd buried himself in her intimate heat.

Lord help him, he wanted to do it again despite the secret she'd kept from him all these years. Yet after such a cruel betrayal, how would he ever be able to trust her again?

She settled the boy on the edge of the couch. His legs swung back and forth in perpetual motion.

"Careful now, honey," she said, handing Adam one of the mugs. "The chocolate is hot."

''I tried to cool it off with some cold milk so he wouldn't burn his tongue.'' Shoving the magazines aside, Rory sat on the coffee table in front of Adam, waiting until the boy had his first taste of hot chocolate. Or maybe he was waiting because he didn't know the words to use.

''You remember how I told you I used to visit your grandma Justy when I was young?'' Kristi began, taking the lead.

The boy nodded. Rory was glad she'd figured out a way to start.

''That's when I met your mom,'' Rory said.

''Were you just kids like me?''

''No. Older than that. Grown up.'' At the time, Rory had thought of himself as a responsible adult. In retrospect, it didn't look as if he'd done a very good job of it.

''Rory and I started to like each other. A lot.'' She stroked the back of her son's head, but her eyes were on Rory. ''Sometimes when a man and woman care about each other, they—''

She hesitated, unsure of what to say next, and Rory definitely didn't want her to go into specifics about what he and Kristi had done that summer.

''Adam, I'm your father.''

The boy dipped his finger into the hot chocolate to snare a marshmallow. Thoughtfully, he licked his finger clean. For the first time since he'd sat down his legs stopped swinging back and forth.

The silence in the room was deafening. Rory was afraid to breathe, and he guessed Kristi was, too. The only sound came from a four-wheel-drive vehicle passing by on the main road, the snow tires humming on the hard-packed snow.

"Honey, do you understand what Rory is saying?"

The youngster looked up at his mother. "Like he's my *real* dad?"

"Yes, that's right, honey. Rory is your father. Remember how we talked about a man planting a seed inside a mommy's tummy, and then she gets to have a baby to love?"

His legs started in motion again. "If he's my dad, how come he doesn't live with us?"

This was the hard part, the unforgivable part, Rory thought. "I didn't know until this afternoon that you existed, son, that your mom had had you."

Tiny furrows formed across the boy's forehead, and he glanced up at his mother. "Did you forget to tell him, Mom?"

She pursed her lips, and tears glistened in her eyes. "Something like that."

"But I know now," Rory said. "And I'm really glad you're my son."

"Are you gonna come live with Mom and me and Grandma?"

"This is Rory's home," Kristi hastily interjected. "Here in Montana."

"Then how can he be my dad if he doesn't live with us?"

"We, uh, haven't quite worked out the details yet, son," Rory said. He hadn't even begun to think that far ahead. "But you can be sure you and I will be spending a lot of time together. We need to get to know each other, right?"

"I guess." Tipping his head back, he drained the cup of hot chocolate. "Can I tell Troy you're my dad?"

"Sure. Who's Troy?"

"He's Adam's best friend at school." Kristi took the cup from the boy and placed it on the table.

"Sometimes Troy says I'm dorky cuz I don't have a dad like he does. Now I can tell him I do."

"Yeah, you can." Rory's throat tightened, and a painful band constricted his chest. His son had been teased because he hadn't been there for the boy. Rory remembered similar incidents as a kid that had only become worse when he'd been hooked into the foster care system. Getting teased or bullied wasn't going to happen again to his son. Not ever.

Adam hopped down from the couch. "Can I go call Troy now, Mom? Can I?"

"Why don't you wait till we get back home?"

"But I wanna tell him *now*," Adam demanded. He scrunched his face in a mulish mask.

Kristi remained firm but calm. "We'll do it when we get home."

A full-fledged temper tantrum threatened, the boy silently challenging his mother. Rory wanted to step in to head off the problem, and cursed himself because he didn't know what approach would work best with Adam. Or if anything would help.

Because he didn't know his son.

Because he didn't know how to be a father.

The boy glowered at his mother, then darted a look at Rory as though in search of support.

Rory was tempted to offer his phone. He didn't

want this Troy kid to ever have a chance to tease his son again. But he couldn't undermine Kristi's relationship with the boy.

"It would probably be better to tell your friend in person," Rory said.

Adam didn't look entirely mollified. He gave a sullen shrug, whirled and ran out the back. The house shook when the door slammed behind him.

Coming to his feet, Rory went to the window and watched his son run across the road to Doc Justine's place. He'd forgotten his jacket on the couch, and his white sweatshirt made him almost invisible against the snow. Rory's heart lunged in his chest. It was almost as though the boy had vanished from Rory's life as quickly as he had appeared, becoming nothing more than a ghost.

Then the youngster popped up onto Justine's porch, his blue jeans dark against the wood siding, and he flew into the house. Even from across the street Rory could hear the door bang shut behind the boy.

He turned to Kristi. "Will he be all right?"

She still sat on the couch, her hands wrapped around her mug of chocolate that had now turned cold. She studied the cup as though it contained the answers to the world's most complex problems. "Adam can be stubborn, and he does have a problem with his temper and impulse control, but he seemed to accept the fact that you're his father."

A muscle twitched in Rory's jaw. "If he was being goaded by his friend about not having a dad, how could you not have told Adam about me?"

"I didn't know he was being teased. He never said anything."

"Maybe you should have figured it isn't easy to not have a dad."

She lifted her head. Her eyes were filled with so much pain, he had to steel himself against the sympathy that rose up in him. "He has friends whose parents are divorced, the fathers not living at home."

"But those kids know who their dads are, don't they?"

Her head dipped in acknowledgment that what he'd said was true. "What are we going to do now? About Adam, I mean."

Exhaling, he tried to ease some of the tension from his shoulders by lifting them and rotating his neck. "I honestly don't know. I haven't fully absorbed the fact that I'm a father." Or that Kristi had kept that secret from him for so many years. It wasn't easy to take a double punch to the solar plexus and recover quickly.

"I know you're angry with me and maybe you have a right to be. But look at it from my perspective. At least I *tried* to reach you, tell you I was pregnant. You never even bothered to send me a letter."

"I've explained about school—"

"What we shared that summer couldn't have meant all that much to you since you made no effort to stay in touch. If anything, our guilt flows both ways, Rory. You've been out of school for how many years and you've never lifted a finger to try to find out what happened to me."

Rory cursed himself because what she said was

true. At first he didn't feel he'd had anything to offer her, and then he'd been afraid to find out that she'd found someone else. Not very good excuses, not when he considered his son.

In response to his silence, she picked up Adam's jacket and stood. "I'd planned to stay with Grandma Justine for two weeks. By then Grandma should be able to manage on her own. I'll have to go back to work. That's all the vacation time I have."

Two weeks, and the better part of four days had already gone by. That's all the time she was allowing him to get to know his son. Dammit, that wasn't enough!

"I'll want to spend as much time as possible with him while he's here," Rory said.

"Of course." She crossed the room toward the kitchen and stopped. "If it matters to you, I cried myself to sleep every night for months when I thought you'd found someone else."

Yes, it mattered. But it didn't change the fact he'd missed the first five years of his son's life.

"Whatever we decide to do," she said, "I don't want Adam hurt."

Rory nodded. There seemed to be enough hurt to go around for everyone to share.

KRISTI'S THOUGHTS weighed heavily on her as she followed Adam's small boot prints across the road to her grandmother's house. Her son had been taunted because of her mistakes. Now he was at risk of becoming even more confused by parents who lived hundreds of miles apart.

She should be grateful that Rory hadn't rejected his son. In fact, he seemed ready to offer his unconditional love. But with Rory's instant acceptance of the boy came the threat of a custody dispute not unlike the one her girlfriend had to endure.

"God, what a mess I've made," she said aloud. She swiped at a new wave of tears that flooded her eyes.

The sound of a fast-moving vehicle on the snow behind her made her start. She scooted to the side of the driveway as a pickup roared up to the clinic entrance. Almost before it stopped, the driver leaped out, a woman, and she hurried around to the passenger side.

Responding to her training, Kristi's thoughts immediately shifted to handling whatever the emergency might be. She reached the truck as the woman began helping a man out of the cab. However much Kristi wanted to talk with her son, make sure he was all right and understood about Rory, she knew her first responsibility was to a patient in trouble. For now, both Adam and her emotional dilemma could wait. Neither qualified as an emergency.

"I'm Kristi Kerrigan, Doc Justine's granddaughter," she said calmly, aiding the gentleman to his feet. His left hand was wrapped in a white, blood-soaked towel. "What happened?"

"He cut his fingers on the chain saw," the woman explained.

"We had some trees downed in the storm." A man of about sixty, he clutched his injured hand to his chest. He had the look of a rancher, his faced lined and deeply tanned. But now he appeared pale beneath that tan, probably from shock and loss of blood. "Fool thing jammed on me."

"Well, let's get you inside and we'll take a look at what we have here."

"We thought we'd see Doc Justine," the woman said. She, too, showed evidence of having lived in Montana for the better part of her life, her face as aged as her husband's and now pinched with worry.

"I'm assisting her for a few days. I'm a nurse practitioner. Your husband will be just fine, Mrs...."

"Lovell. I'm Barb and this is Charlie."

Kristi hustled the couple inside and to an examining room. "Why don't you sit right here, Mr. Lovell," she told the gentleman, "and we'll take a look at what we've got." She knew without looking that the patient would need stitches. It remained to be seen if a more complicated procedure would be required for him to retain the full use of his hand.

Once the patient was seated, Kristi shrugged out of her jacket and began scrubbing her hands in the nearby sink. Wearing gloves, she set out her instruments on a sterile tray—syringe, lidocaine, hemostat. She'd performed this task a thousand times at the Spokane clinic and before that at a big city hospital. There was no end to the ways people could injure themselves, from knives to cracking their skulls by standing up too fast beneath an overhanging shelf.

"My hand hurts like hell, miss. If you could get the doctor—"

"She'll be right here." Kristi was confident Justine

had heard their arrival. "And as soon as she takes a look, I'll get you something to stop that pain."

The thump of Doc Justine's crutches preceded her arrival in the examining room. "Well, Charlie, what'd you do this time?"

"Looks like you got more troubles than I do," he said, checking out Justine's cast.

"Careful, youngster, I can still run circles around you if I have to."

Kristi stepped back while Justine, leaning on her crutches, unwrapped the injured hand. She flushed the wound with normal-saline solution and took a good look at the damaged fingertips. Only a small amount of blood continued to ooze from the injury. Her examination didn't take long.

"Looks like you'll live, Charlie, but you won't be playing the guitar for a while." Justine draped a sterile cloth over the injury. "I'm gonna have my granddaughter stitch you up. Then she'll give you a tetanus shot, since you've been keeping your distance from me the past few years."

"You're the one who's always sewed me up before." Charlie eyed Kristi dubiously.

"Kristi does some real pretty needlework, and my hand isn't as steady as it used to be." Justine nodded for Kristi to take over. "She'll do you up fancy enough to show your fingers off at the county fair along with those award-winning quilts Barb makes."

Barb looked relieved her husband's injury wasn't too severe. Grimacing from the pain, Charlie didn't appear quite so confident.

At ease with her abilities, Kristi pulled a rolling

stool into position in front of Charlie. What surprised her was Justine's admission that she wasn't as steady as she used to be. Maybe her age was finally catching up with Justine.

Maybe Kristi's grandmother needed an assistant for more than a couple of weeks.

Kristi filled a syringe with lidocaine. While she waited for the painkiller to take effect, she took Charlie's blood pressure and a brief medical history. Then she slipped into clean gloves and went to work. It was nearly an hour before she finished her suturing task, repairing three fingertips. She gave Charlie a tetanus shot and sent the couple off to see Harold Hudson at the local pharmacy with a prescription from Justine for pain pills.

After she cleaned up the examining room, she went in search of Adam. She found Grandma Justine and Dottie in the kitchen fixing hamburgers for supper. Expecting Adam to be hanging out near them in the hope of cookies and milk, she glanced around the warm, inviting room that smelled of meat sizzling on the stove.

"Where's Adam?" she asked.

"He came in just before you and the Lovells arrived," Justine said.

"I think he went upstairs, dear." Dottie stood at the counter slicing tomatoes. "He said something about calling home, to Spokane, but I told him he couldn't use Grandma Justy's phone to make a long-distance call."

Kristi's forehead tightened in a frown. Adam had been so determined to tell Troy about...

Anxiety prickled at the nape of her neck, and a chill ran down her spine. "I'll go upstairs and see what he's up to."

She forced herself to remain calm as she climbed the stairs. Adam was as likely to be playing with his Rocket Rangers as anything else. Or maybe he'd discovered a new game to play on Justine's computer. When he set his mind to it, he was quite proficient for his age on a computer.

She checked the guest room where she'd slept the night of her arrival, and then she peered into the room where Dottie had unpacked her bags. Her pace increasing, she nearly sprinted down the hallway to Justine's room and her adjacent sunroom, which she used as an upstairs office. The computer was dark. No sign of her son.

"Adam!" she called. She remembered dozens of nooks and crannies in the old house where a child could hide—from the attic to the basement. Trying to keep her panic at bay, she began to methodically search each room. She called her son's name over and over, but there was no response. Soon her mother joined her in the search.

"I can't imagine where's he gone," Dottie complained. "If I'd thought he was going to be so upset about the phone call—"

"It's all right, Mom. He can't have gone far." She glanced outside into the deepening twilight, praying that was true. Surely her son hadn't been so distraught that he'd even consider—

Across the way she spotted Rory forking hay into an outdoor pen. Surely if Adam wasn't in the house he'd gone there, to Rory's, to see the wolf that had so fascinated him. Or maybe to hang out with his newfound father.

She sprinted for the stairs.

"Kristi, where are you going?" her mother cried.

"To find my son."

She didn't bother with her jacket. Or boots. She simply raced out the front door and across the road, arriving breathless at Rory's side.

"What's wrong?" he asked immediately.

"Adam. I can't find him. Is he here with you?"

A stillness fell over Rory that filled Kristi with dread, and his eyes narrowed. "I haven't seen him since before you left my place. Isn't he at Doc's house?"

Icy cold seeped into Kristi's bones, sending icicles of fear into her soul, and she hugged herself.

"He wanted to use Grandma Justy's phone to call Troy. Mother told him no."

Rory's gaze swept the landscape, taking in everything from the stores on Main Street with their lights glowing through the rapidly chilling air to the passing truck on the road. A woman hurried into the general store, she'd probably forgotten some important ingredient for tonight's dinner. Metal banged on metal at the garage, a dented fender getting straightened with muscle power rather than finesse.

Rory swallowed hard. *Where was his son?*

"Could he just run off like that?" he asked, bewildered and more filled with a gut-wrenching fear than he'd ever imagined possible.

"I don't know." Visibly, it was an effort for Kristi

to keep hold of herself and her emotions. "He can be impulsive. His teacher thinks he has ADD, that he ought to be on medication."

"That's crazy. He's just an ordinary kid." An active, possibly excitable kid who'd gone missing. Rory bit back a curse.

"I agree. But he's gone, Rory. I can't find him anywhere." Her voice sounded poised on the edged of hysteria.

Rory shoved his pitchfork into a pile of hay. "I'll find him."

"How?"

"He's a little kid. How far could he get on his own?"

Rory didn't want to consider how many times he'd run away from foster homes. But he'd been older than Adam and far more rebellious. Or so he hoped. And more times than not, some cop had hauled him back to his foster home before he'd gone more than a few miles. Except one time he'd managed to hitch a ride to the neighboring town.

"First thing," Rory said, "I'm going to ask Eric to help us find Adam. He'll know what to do. Then we'll go looking ourselves."

TILTING HIS DESK CHAIR forward, Eric studied Kristi in surprise. "I didn't know you had a son."

"Adam is my son, too," Rory announced.

Eric's head snapped around so fast he almost fell out of his chair. It would have been funny if Kristi weren't so worried about Adam.

"He's gone off somewhere," Kristi said. "I can't find him. Rory thought you could help us look."

"Yeah, sure." Eric's inquisitive gaze darted from Kristi to Rory and back again. "How long have you…I mean, after all this time—"

"It's getting dark, bro. The details can come later. For now can you do an all-points bulletin or something?"

"Let's start from the beginning." Eric seemed to shake off his questions—for the moment. "I'll need a description of the boy, what he was wearing, how long he's been missing. Kristi, why don't you begin? When did you last see him?" He arranged a yellow pad on the desk and waited.

Shivering despite the comfortable temperature in the sheriff's office, Kristi related what had transpired that afternoon. She tried to hurry through the details so they could get on with the search, but Eric insisted upon being thorough. She clenched her teeth in frustration, answering his questions as best she could.

Meanwhile, Rory paced the office, frequently glancing out the window.

"Look, I'm going to check around town," Rory said. "Maybe somebody has seen him."

Relieved Rory was ready to take some action, Kristi said, "I'm coming with you."

Eric pulled a handheld radio from a desk drawer and tossed it to his brother. "Keep in touch with this. While you're checking in town, I'll notify the state police. If Joe Moore is at the dry goods store, ask him to check the roads north of here. I'll take the patrol car south to the highway."

Kristi gasped. "He couldn't have gone that far, could he?"

Eric shrugged. "Kids have amazing endurance when they're trying to run away. And if someone has picked him up…"

He left the thought unfinished, and Kristi shuddered. Dear God, something awful could have happened to her son. The news was always filled with children who were missing and were never found.

She glanced at Rory and found his eyes on her, dark and filled with the same fear and worry that snaked through her. He'd only just discovered his son, and now he could lose him.

They could *both* lose Adam.

Rory straightened his Stetson on his head and placed an encouraging hand on Kristi's shoulder. "Let's roll. We'll find the boy."

Chapter Ten

"It's so cold. What if we don't find—" Kristi's voice cracked.

"Don't even think it," Rory said grimly. He shrugged out of his heavy sheepskin jacket and slipped it around Kristi's slender shoulders. They'd been into every store and shop in town, and searched through the back alleys. No one had seen Adam. He'd simply vanished from the face of the earth. All they'd accomplished was to let the entire town of Grass Valley in on the news that he and Kristi had a son. "We need to get you back to the house and warmed up. Then we can—"

"I'm going to keep looking until I know he's safe."

"You're freezing. At least you need your jacket."

Frantically, she looked up and down Main Street. Her usually neat hair was a mess from her running her fingers through it. In the faint light from the drugstore window, he could see bruises of fear and fatigue under her eyes. They'd been searching for more than an hour and still this slight, stubborn woman wouldn't quit. He doubted she'd ever give up.

If it hadn't been for his tutor answering the phone, lying to Kristi, she wouldn't have quit on him.

"Come on." He took her hand. "We'll use my truck and check the road out of town." At least the truck heater would keep them both warm while they continued the search.

"I thought Eric and Mr. Moore were doing that."

"Maybe they missed him. I don't know." He remembered how little Adam had looked running across the road to the doctor's house. It wouldn't take a very big bush to hide the boy from sight. Or a very deep ditch to swallow him up. "I've got this gut feeling that Adam decided he'd walk back home so he could thumb his nose at Troy about having a dad. That's what I would have done."

"But it's hundreds of miles back to Spokane," she protested.

"You and I know that, but I doubt a five-year-old can fully grasp that kind of detail."

He got her into his SUV and cranked up the heater as soon as the engine had warmed. Once they were underway, his headlights cut a narrow swath through the darkness, glancing off patches of snow along the side of the road in the moonless night.

"Hit that floodlight on your side of the truck," he instructed. He'd installed floodlights on both sides of the cab, using them when he searched for injured animals at night. He hadn't expected to be hunting for his own son. "Train it along the ditch. Maybe we'll spot something."

He drove slowly, scanning both sides of the plowed road, a black stripe of asphalt between two mounded piles of snow, and he peered through the shadowy landscape. He knew from tracking injured animals how hard it was to spot a lone figure in the darkness. A deer could look like a tree, a child like a scrub bush or a motionless rock beside the road.

The knot in his stomach pressed on his breast bone, making it difficult to breathe.

He picked up the radio microphone from the console beside him and squeezed to transmit. "Eric, anything yet?"

A second's pause and his brother responded. "Not yet. I'm about five miles out of town to the west. I'll turn around now."

Kristi said, "Adam couldn't go that far. He's just a little boy." The threat of tears filled her quavering voice. She worked the floodlight back and forth along the edge of the road.

"We're two miles south," Rory responded on the radio. "We'll keep looking." He tried to think like a kid. A kid who had to be cold and tired by now. A kid who needed a father.

"I had Joe call the outlying ranches. We've got everybody checking the roads near them, and Harold is starting another search in town, including Doc Justine's house, in case the boy's hiding inside. Tell Kristi we'll find him. Try not to worry."

"Easier said than done, bro." His gaze scanned the shoulder of the road. The piles of plowed snow were beginning to look old, which meant not even a footprint would be apparent, assuming there were any.

"There!" Kristi cried. "It's Adam!"

Rory followed the light. A hundred yards ahead of them a tiny figure trudged alongside the road.

"Thank God!" he whispered in both prayer and thanksgiving. He grabbed the mike again. "We've got him, Eric. We've got him."

A dozen voices filled the airwaves with expressions of relief and thanks.

He eased up near the boy and stopped to let Kristi out. She ran to her son, scooping him into her arms, hugging him.

Breathing deeply, Rory rested his forehead on the steering wheel. The sob that racked his chest and the warm tears that dampened his cheeks surprised him. He hadn't cried since he was eight years old and realized he would never see his mother again.

KRISTI'S TEETH were chattering uncontrollably by the time she and Rory got Adam into her lap in the SUV. The adrenaline that had kept her going for the past few hours drained away, leaving her chilled to the bone. But her son was safe. Nothing else mattered. She would have willingly walked across frozen tundra to find him, and now she vowed she'd never let him go.

"Mom, you're squishing me," Adam complained.

She adjusted her position as Rory wrapped a blanket around both her and Adam. Warm air blew full blast from the SUV's heater.

"You could do with a little squishing after running off like that," she said.

"Are you mad at me?" His eyebrows pulled together above troubled dark eyes.

"No, I'm not mad. I'm upset and disappointed, and I was worried sick. What if we hadn't found you? You know how important you are to me."

"I was coming back after I told Troy about my dad."

Kristi shivered. Long before Adam reached Spokane he would have died of hypothermia. If it weren't for his stubborn determination to reach his destination, Adam might have already succumbed to the cold.

She glanced at Rory as he climbed into the truck. He slammed the door behind him but left the overhead light on. Rory had shown the same sort of determination by completing veterinary school in the face of his dyslexia and long odds. Apparently, he'd passed that stubborn gene on to his son.

Rory cupped the back of Adam's head with his hand, and she noted the fine tremble of his fingers. His cheeks were pale, his eyes bloodshot and puffy as though he'd been crying. For the first time, the black Stetson he wore didn't make him appear dangerous. Now he looked as vulnerable as she felt.

Her heart filled with an understanding of the depth of his love for his son.

"He's going to be okay?" he asked.

She nodded and tried to find her voice. "He appears to be in better shape than either of us."

"Heck of a thing, huh?" His arm encompassing

both Adam and Kristi, Rory tugged them into a tight circle until his head was resting on hers. She felt as much as heard the deep sigh that shuddered through him. She echoed his sense of relief.

At an even deeper level she experienced a feeling of *rightness*. That this was how they were meant to be—a family.

In the dim interior of the SUV yet another emotion pressed in on her, taking up space around her heart and leaving her trembling.

Fear.

It tore at her spirits, threatening to snatch away hopes and dreams that had only just been reawakened. It made her afraid that it was too late to erase past mistakes and move into the future with the only man she had ever loved—ever *could* love.

From beneath the blanket, Adam sputtered, "Hey, I can't breathe down here."

Lifting his head, Rory gave Kristi a wry grin. "How 'bout we go back to town? I don't think it's too late for Adam to make that phone call he's been so worried about."

"Can we eat first?" Adam asked. "I'm real hungry."

"Whatever you want, champ," Kristi said. "As long as you promise you won't run off again without telling Mommy where you're going."

"'Kay." He snuggled against her, unaware that he'd put both Kristi and Rory through an emotional wringer by his sudden disappearance.

She wondered if Rory had any idea of the depth of pain she'd suffered at his hands, intended or not, or if he was equally oblivious. Maybe that was simply how men were wired. They dealt with the present and left the repercussions to others.

He fastened his seat belt and wheeled the truck into a U-turn, heading back toward town. Even though the roads were slick with snow melt turning to icy patches, he drove with easy confidence. His strong fingers curled around the steering wheel in an almost sensual caress—a caress Kristi longed to experience again.

From the beginning Rory had been able to reach her at some elemental level. He was the fantasy of her early adolescence, dark and dangerous in an exotic way. His body lean and sensual. His voice enough to curl her toes, the way he looked at her tantalizing her imagination.

That summer in Grass Valley, her fantasy had come alive in glorious living color and warm provocative flesh, and she'd been charged with all the sexual attraction she'd dreamed about. Her usual reserve with men had spiraled out of control. At the time, she'd thought the seduction had been mutual. Despite the absence of vows, she'd believed he loved her as much as she loved him.

And then the summer ended, she'd gone home to Spokane filled with hope and plans for the future, only to have them shattered when she discovered she was pregnant.

Swallowing the memories, she rubbed her hand up and down Adam's back as he cuddled on her lap.

How could she possibly risk having Rory hurt her again? Despite resolving some of their misunderstandings, the wound he'd inflicted had been so deep it still hadn't entirely healed. And now she had Adam's future to consider. His well-being, both emotional and physical.

She knew a boy needed a father. But the thought of agreeing to a two-state custody arrangement was unbearable. Her job, her roots and the life she'd built for herself and her son were in Spokane. Grass Valley represented the only stable home Rory had ever experienced. She couldn't demand that he leave all of that in order to be with his son.

And never once, not even during their summer together, had he mentioned marriage. He'd only said a long-term relationship probably wouldn't work.

He'd been right.

A long-distance relationship between father and son wouldn't be much easier.

IT LOOKED AS THOUGH Grandma Justine was playing host to a meeting of the Cattlemen's Association. Four-wheel-drive pickups and SUVs were parked everywhere, most of the trucks sporting a rifle in a rack across the back of the cab. All of the vehicles were mud spattered, and a good many of them had dented fenders. People were still arriving, husbands and wives, even young children bundled up in their robes and slippers to be carried inside.

"What's going on?" Kristi asked.

Rory turned into his own driveway, which was less crowded than Grandma Justine's property. "Looks like a few neighbors from the rescue team showed up to welcome Adam home safely."

Alerted to the excitement, Adam straightened and peered out the window. "They've all come to see me?"

"Looks like it, champ." Rory ruffled the boy's already mussed hair. "Guess you're a celebrity."

"What's a sell-a-brit?"

"Somebody important." Rory popped open his door and hopped out.

Mentally, Kristi groaned. She hadn't anticipated a welcoming party. She'd only wanted to feed Adam and get him settled back into some sort of routine.

"Wow!" Squirming around, Adam let himself out of the truck in a hurry. He raced to where Rory waited for him and took his father's hand. They headed across the road.

Kristi followed more slowly. She dreaded meeting all of these people. From the search and radio communication, everyone now knew that she'd had Rory's son. She had no idea what kind of reception she'd get. If they would condemn her for what she'd done. Whose side they'd take.

Still, she had an obligation to thank them for their efforts to find Adam when he'd run off. They'd interrupted their own lives to search for her son. Despite her trepidation, she couldn't ignore them.

Lifting her chin and squaring her shoulders, she stepped inside the open door to her grandmother's house. The decibel level was extraordinarily high as people clustered around Adam, welcoming him home.

Hetty Moore was the first to spot Kristi standing in the entryway.

"My sakes, child. You must have been so frightened when your boy ran off." Hetty embraced her as warmly as though Kristi were her own daughter. "I remember when my middle one decided to walk to Disneyland because we didn't have the money to take her. They can break a mama's heart, can't they?"

Kristi was barely able to acknowledge Hetty's remarks with a nod before Marlene Huhn and Valery Haywood added their hugs and encouragement.

"Young Adam looks so like our Rory, don't you think? So handsome." Marlene said. "You must be very proud of the boy, ja?"

"Yes, I am."

"And Rory such a fine man," Valery added. "You're a lucky woman, that's what I think."

Kristi smiled feebly and tried to make her way to her son, who'd been swallowed up by the male portion of the search team. Before she could reach Adam, a flaxen-haired blonde about her own age who was carrying a rosy-cheeked baby in her arms stopped Kristi.

"Hi, I'm Lizzie Oakes, Walker's wife. We're so glad you found your boy." Lizzie's daughter, who looked to be about a year old, gazed at her with eyes the same dramatic shade of blue as her mother's.

"Thank you." Kristi spoke the words automatically before recognition set in. "Oh! You're Rory's sister-in-law."

"And this is Susie-Q." Lizzie hugged her daughter. "I gather, from what's being said around town, that being married to Walker makes me Adam's aunt."

Kristi stumbled over a response. She hadn't been prepared for an instant family reunion.

"I do hope you'll bring Adam around to visit the ranch. If he likes horses, he'll love the Double O, and the boys would love to get acquainted."

"Boys?"

"Walker and I are in the process of adopting four teenage boys he had in foster care."

"Oh, yes, Rory told me about that. You're a very courageous woman to take on so many children, particularly adolescents. One more and you'll be able to field your own basketball team."

Lizzie grimaced then smiled. "Please don't suggest that to Walker. He'd probably love the idea."

Chuckling, Kristi said, "My lips are sealed."

Laughter erupted from the clutch of men around Adam, and the baby squirmed around in her mother's arms to see what was happening.

"Hey, Mom, these guys say they're my cousins," Adam shouted. "Cool, huh? I never had cousins before." One of the young men, who was built like a linebacker, hefted Adam in his arms.

"That's Fridge," Lizzie explained. Despite the woman's informal name and ease with being a mother of a large brood of disparate children, Kristi detected an undercurrent of sophistication. "Our middle son. He's a whiz at anything mechanical. The redhead is Scotty. He's the best baby-sitter you can imagine, if you ever need one. That's his younger sister, Nancy, who he's lugging around. She's a sweetie pie and adores all the boys. We're adopting her, too." She smiled fondly at the pair.

"And the tall, slender boy is String Bean. He's still getting used to the size of his feet and tends to stumble over them more times than not. But on horseback, he's a wonder. The shorter boy with dark hair is Frankie. He's from Chicago and recently took up the trumpet. That's been a, shall we say, challenging experience."

Susie made a determined effort to pinch her mother's nose. Lizzie took the baby's hand and gently gnawed on her fingers with her lips. "And that big, handsome fellow in the sheepskin coat is my husband, Walker."

"Yes, I remember him from my visit to Grass Valley some years ago, although I spent most of my time with Rory." And it was all too obvious what she and Rory had been doing. "I'm in awe of both you and Walker. I'm not at all sure I could handle that many adolescents even one at a time."

Lizzie laughed lightly. "They're really good boys. The only problem is keeping them fed. Besides, adopting them is Walker's way of paying back what Oliver Oakes did for him and Eric and Rory."

"I can understand that." Kristi recalled that all three of the brothers had been adopted, an extraordinary gift, and no doubt part of the reason Rory was now so intent on becoming involved in Adam's life.

He wanted a family of his own.

"Rory is a pretty terrific uncle, by the way. So is Eric, for that matter. Despite their rocky beginnings, they've all grown up to be fine men."

"Yes, that's true," Kristi agreed. After all the anxiety of searching for Adam, it was a struggle to remember what Rory had told her about Walker and Lizzie's history. "How long have you and Walker been married?"

"About six months." She caught Kristi's quick glance at Lizzie's daughter, who was obviously older than that. "Susie-Q and I showed up on Walker's doorstep one day, much to his surprise. I coaxed him into hiring me as his housekeeper, which was a real stretch. And the rest, as they say, is history."

She nodded, remembering more of the story. "So Susie isn't Walker's real daughter, either?"

"She is now." Lizzie spoke with both pride and love for the man she'd married just as Walker arrived at her side.

With a happy giggle, Susie lunged for her daddy.

"Hey, princess." He caught the baby and gave her a little toss in the air, which elicited another round of baby laughter. "Missed your old man, huh?"

He winked at his wife, then leaned down to brush a brotherly kiss to Kristi's cheek. "I always did think Rory would be one lucky Indian chief if he landed you."

Kristi flushed with embarrassment. "Things didn't quite work out like either of us expected."

"Who knows. Maybe there's still time. Love can pop up when you least expect it. Marriage, too." He gave his wife an intimate look that would have made any woman blush with pleasure. Lizzie was no exception, and her cheeks blossomed with color.

"I hope you don't mind," Walker said. "I invited Adam out to the ranch if he gets a chance. The boys will give him a riding lesson. You're more than welcome, too.''

"Your wife already extended the invitation. Thank you.''

"Please do come,'' Lizzie insisted. "With all the men around the house, I sometimes get lonely for a woman to talk to.''

"I don't plan to stay in town long. Just until my grandmother is more comfortable getting around on her own. But I'll make it a point to visit the Double O.'' An only child, Kristi wasn't used to a big family or their warm welcome. But it was obvious Adam was tickled to discover he had so many relatives.

"Bring ol' Bird Brain with you,'' Walker suggested.

She frowned, puzzled. "Bird Brain?'' That's a term she'd heard Walker use on the radio at the cabin when she'd been eavesdropping. She'd wondered…

"Rory's Blackfeet Indian name is Swift Eagle, which Eric and I thought was way too elegant for our little brother,'' Walker explained.

"I see.'' Apparently Walker made it a habit to give nicknames to everyone in his family. She wondered what he might dub her, *if* she remained in Grass Valley for any length of time.

"Anyway, the cows are beginning to drop their calves now, and he can check them out while you visit with Lizzie.'' He slid his free arm around his wife's waist. "We better head on home. I saw Fridge wander into Doc Justine's kitchen. He'll clean out her refrigerator if we don't get him out of there.''

Lizzie agreed with her husband, adding that it was

time for Susie-Q and little Nancy to be in bed. ''We just wanted to be here to celebrate Adam being found. And, of course, we were a little curious to meet you. Rory is an important part of our family. We hope his son will be, too.''

''I'm sure we'll be able to work out something.'' Although at this point, Kristi couldn't be sure what the arrangements might be.

She glanced around, spotting Rory on the far side of the room talking with Eric. In spite of the crowd of people, her stomach did a little flip-flop and her heart skipped a beat. She suspected no matter how many years passed, she'd always react strongly to the sight of him.

In contrast, despite the caring way he'd made love to her at the cabin, she couldn't read his feelings now. Not since the revelation that he had a son.

EVENTUALLY THE TOWNSPEOPLE went home and Justine's house cleared out. Dottie Kerrigan reheated a chicken-and-rice casserole in the microwave and rounded up Adam, Rory and Kristi for a late supper.

''Mom, did you know I'm an Indian?'' Adam asked with his mouth full of chicken and rice.

''Yes, I knew.'' Adam had never been curious about his ancestry before he met Rory so the subject had never come up. ''You're also part Irish from the Kerrigan side of the family and part French from the Beauchamps.'' In all the excitement and stress, Kristi's appetite had fled. Halfheartedly she forked a piece of chicken into her mouth.

''Do I gots any Irish cousins?''

"Not that I know of."

"My dad's all Indian, aren't you?" He checked with his father.

"I don't actually know because I don't know who my father was. But my mother was mostly Indian."

"Blackfeet?" Kristi asked. She'd never bothered to ask. His tribal background meant little to her six years ago. Now, because of her son, she was sorry she hadn't paid more attention to the details of Rory's family history. But then, he hadn't been exactly forthcoming. And they'd had other things to do with their time rather than chatting about their respective ancestries.

"Probably. At least the tribe has accepted me as a member. My mother never mentioned her tribe that I can remember."

Adam lifted his foot and started taking off his boot.

"What are you doing, dear?" Dottie had seated herself at the end of the table near the stove after serving up the dinner plates. "You know we don't take off our shoes at the table," she admonished the boy.

"I'm tryin' to see if my feet are black, too, like my dad's."

Kristi winced, and Rory chuckled.

"That's not exactly how it works." He smiled at his son. "Blackfeet is the name the white men gave to a particular group of Indians they chased into Montana."

"How come they chased 'em here?"

Kristi held up her hand to stop the conversation.

"Let's handle the history lesson another time. Adam needs to eat some supper and then it's bedtime."

"Aw, Mom…"

"Your mother is right, champ. You've had a busy day. We'll talk about the Blackfeet Indians another time."

Looking reasonably mollified, the boy took another bite of dinner. "I get to call Troy before I go to bed, don't I, Mom?"

She checked her watch. Knowing it was an hour earlier in Spokane than Grass Valley, she decided it wasn't too late for Adam to make the call. This time she wasn't going to refuse her son's request. "As soon as you finish with your dinner, you may call Troy," she promised.

"Okay." He spilled a good many grains of rice trying to get his overfilled fork to his mouth.

"In the morning you can come visit me and the wolf, if you'd like," Rory suggested before glancing at Kristi. "And maybe we can check out the Double O Ranch, if your mom thinks it's all right."

"Wow, can I? Uncle Eric said my cousin String Bean will teach me to ride a horse and stuff. Can I, huh?"

Everything was moving too fast for Kristi. Her little boy had taken to thinking of Rory as his dad as easily as a youngster developed a taste for sweets. Now he was being swept up into Rory's family. Yet she couldn't object. That wouldn't be fair to her son. Or to Rory.

But she also didn't plan to let Adam go alone to the ranch with Rory. After tonight, the thought of letting Adam out of her sight for even a short time made her feel sick to her stomach.

How could she ever agree to sharing custody of her son with anyone—including the boy's father—when he lived hundreds of miles away?

Chapter Eleven

By morning Rory had reached two decisions: the injured elk he'd rescued was ready to return to his herd, and Rory was going to make Adam his son in every way possible. He didn't think Kristi would fight him about the boy, but he was ready to go to the mat for Adam.

As he used a couple of lead ropes to move the elk from his pen into a horse trailer, he spotted Kristi and Adam coming his way.

His breath jammed in his lungs with the force of a thousand-pound elk in rut ramming into him. Not only did he want Adam to be a part of his life.

He wanted Kristi, too. Permanently.

Despite the secret she'd kept from him, his initial reaction of anger and guilt, he still wanted her.

The memory of making love to her at the cabin started a slow burn deep in his gut. How could he not want to feel the weight of her full breasts in his hands again, taste the sweet flavor of her mouth on his once more? Inside his leather gloves, his fingers itched with the memory of her silken hair running through them, how it felt to caress her satin skin. He wanted to experience all of that again. And more.

Her job was in Spokane.

How could he ask her to sacrifice what she'd worked so hard to achieve, particularly when he hadn't been there when she needed him?

As a child he'd been taught he didn't deserve that kind of love. Oliver Oakes had tried to teach him differently. But had anything really changed?

Adam skipped through the snow and half climbed up the chain-link fence around the elk pen. "What're ya doing?"

"I'm going to take the elk back to his herd." He closed the trailer door behind the animal.

"Do we gets to come, too?"

He glanced at Kristi, who had crossed the road at a slower pace, her hands tucked into her jacket pockets. Her hair glistened gold in the morning sun, and the sight made him think of all the hidden treasures he wanted to rediscover.

Could he trust her a second time? Would she trust him?

"Sure," he said, his voice slightly rough with an emotion he tried to keep in check. "The place we're going is sort of on the way to the ranch."

"Cool." The boy launched himself off the fence and stomped through the fast-receding snow to the wolf's pen. He hunkered down, safely a foot away from the fence, and peered into the makeshift den. "You gonna let the wolf go, too?"

"Not yet. His leg has to heal first."

Apparently satisfied with Rory's answer, Adam

studied the wolf with intense concentration, more silent and absorbed than Rory had yet to see the youngster.

Her expression somber, Kristi halted a few feet from the horse trailer, watching her son. "Adam's friend Troy didn't believe him about you."

"What's not to believe?" Pulling the gate closed behind him, Rory squeezed out of the pen past the trailer. The elk's hooves made agitated tapping noises on the trailer's wooden floor.

She lifted her shoulders in a baffled shrug. "Who knows where kids get their ideas. Apparently Troy insisted that if you were Adam's father you'd have to live in Spokane. Adam's now convinced you're moving back home with us."

The air grew thick with surprise and conflicting emotions.

Rory spoke slowly, thoughtfully. "I'm licensed in Montana. I've still got some pretty big outstanding loans on this place, more than it's worth if I tried to sell the practice to someone else. Not that a lot of veterinarians would want to work in this small a town."

"I know. This is your home." *Not mine,* she left unsaid. "Apparently Troy didn't believe Adam is a Blackfeet Indian, either."

Rory swore under his breath. As a kid he'd had trouble accepting who he was. He didn't want that for his son. "This friend of Adam's is a born skeptic, isn't he?"

Her gaze slid away from Rory and back to her son. "It will all work itself out."

Rory wished he had that much faith. For one reason or another, he'd spent the better part of his life swimming upstream. His current problem didn't seem much different, with the none-too-minor exception that he didn't know which way he was supposed to swim.

"I wish Adam's teacher could see him now," Kristi mused, watching the boy sit as still as a statue outside the wolf's pen. "She'd change her mind about him being hyperactive."

"Animals are good for kids, especially wild animals. They teach you patience."

She looked up at Rory, her eyes a deeper blue than the Montana sky. "Is that the lesson they taught you?"

"I'm still learning." At the moment, he didn't feel in the least patient. Instead he was edgy, wanting what he wasn't sure he deserved. Afraid to ask for fear he'd be rejected. Not even a hundred percent convinced what he wanted to do was the right thing.

Lifting his Stetson, he resettled it more firmly on his head. "We'd better get going before the elk gets too agitated. I don't want him to injure himself again."

She nodded and called to her son. "Time to go, Adam."

The boy came running, stumbling over his own feet, falling and popping back up again, his heavy sweater covered with snow.

"I think the wolf likes me," he said breathlessly.

"How did you decide that, son?" Rory asked, brushing snow from the boy's front. Such a small thing, casually touching his son, but until now he'd never been given the chance. He'd miss that more than anything else when Kristi took Adam back to Spokane, and the thought brought a catch to his throat.

"The way he looks at me. He's not scared or nuthin'."

"Maybe he thinks you're his little brother," Rory suggested.

Grinning, Adam tipped his head back and howled up at the sky.

To Rory's surprise, the wolf howled back, and they all laughed.

"Come on, little gray wolf." Rory hooked his arm over his son's shoulder. "Time to get going."

He helped Adam into the back seat of the SUV, then took Kristi's elbow to help her into the passenger side. It was a simple gesture. He hadn't intended it to be anything more than courteous. But the sizzle he felt through several layers of clothing was enough to sear him with desire.

She turned and her eyes locked with his. Her expression filled with a responding intensity that made his blood simmer through his veins. She'd felt it, too. That connection they'd always had. Always would. Whatever else might happen between them, at this elemental level they were a match.

But did he dare try to build a future on that and the fact they'd created a child together?

Unable to sort through his conflicting thoughts, Rory slipped behind the steering wheel. "Is Doc Justine okay on her own at the clinic?"

Kristi snapped her seat belt in place. "There aren't any patient appointments this morning. If Justine needs anything, my mother will take care of it."

Adam poked his head between the two front seats. "Grandma Justy says I wear her out just watching me."

"I don't doubt that for a minute, son." Chuckling, Rory turned the key in the ignition. He could understand how Adam's nonstop energy would try Justine's admittedly limited patience. It didn't seem to bother Kristi, though. She was a good mother, he realized. It couldn't have been easy for her, going to school or working full-time and raising the boy— even if she had the help of her parents.

He'd have to thank her for doing such a good job with his son.

ADAM LOOKED SO SMALL sitting on top of the sorrel mare, Kristi could barely resist the urge to drag him out of the corral and into the safety of her arms. The fact that String Bean had a firm grip on the horse's halter—or that three-year-old Nancy was riding a similar horse on her own—did little to ease Kristi's anxiety.

Granted, she'd ridden occasionally during her visits to Grass Valley. But seeing her baby perched on that animal's back was a whole different matter. Heavens, at home she made sure Adam wore a helmet when he was riding his two-wheeler. Now, miles above the ground, his only protection was a little blue baseball cap.

"Doesn't it frighten you to have Nancy on that huge animal?" she asked Lizzie.

They were standing outside the corral watching the activity. Walker and Rory as well as Fridge, Frankie and Scotty plus the hired hands were perched on the rail fence, encouraging Adam's progress. An aging border collie lay in a sunny spot near the adjacent barn.

Having such a large audience observing his first riding lesson made Adam the center of attention, and he was relishing the experience. Given half a chance, the Oakes would spoil her son, though Kristi wouldn't think of denying him the chance to build his self-esteem. He needed all the positive encouragement he could get.

"Nancy's been riding almost from the day she arrived here," Lizzie said, "though Walker hasn't let her go on her own outside the corral yet. He's more protective than I am." From her ringside seat in Lizzie's backpack, Susie tugged at her mother's tattered straw hat and babbled nonsense sounds to join in the conversation.

Lizzie responded with, "I know you want to go on a horsey, sweetie. Maybe later, huh?"

"I suppose Rory thinks you should be grateful Susie isn't riding, too."

"Oh, she does ride," Lizzie said with a laugh. "So far only on her daddy's lap or mine, but she loves it. A few more months and we'll have her riding on her own. Then Walker says we'll have to look for a pony for the girls."

"In that case, you'd better get two. I can't imagine they'll want to share."

Lizzie chuckled. "You make a good point."

When they had arrived at the Double O, Kristi had noted how prosperous the ranch appeared. She suspected the white two-story house had been painted within the past year. That and the red barn gleamed in the sunlight as did the tractor parked near the barn. A couple of well-used pickups were showing their age, but she imagined vehicles on a working ranch had a short life expectancy. Fender dings would be the norm.

En route to the ranch she'd seen a herd of healthy cattle, still shaggy with their winter coats, grazing around the few remaining patches of snow.

Walker Oakes, with the help of his rapidly expanding family, appeared to be running a very successful operation.

Her gaze slid to Rory on the far side of the corral, where he was chatting with his brother. From what she'd seen, his veterinary practice would be a success, too. More importantly, she knew he had a passion for working with animals. Healing them. Just as she had wanted to treat human patients.

When Rory had released the elk earlier, he'd watched it lope toward the rest of the herd with the kind of pride she would expect to see in a father's eyes when sending his son off to college.

A band tightened around her chest as she wondered if that would be a moment they would share together with Adam. Or if those special milestones in a child's life would be experienced by only one parent at a time.

She exhaled a troubled sigh.

"Should I offer a penny for your thoughts?" Lizzie asked.

"I'm not sure they're worth that much."

"Is Rory having some trouble adjusting to the idea of being a father?"

Kristi's gaze followed Adam's passage around the corral, String Bean still leading the horse. "Just the opposite. He's far more upset about my having kept Adam from him all these years. Rightfully so, from his point of view." And there was no getting rid of the guilt she still felt, though she hadn't known what else to do.

"I'm sure you did what you thought was best at the time."

"In retrospect, particularly now that I've learned what really happened, I should have tried harder to let Rory know I was pregnant." Even if the news had cost him the career he had dreamed of? she wondered. Would that really have been best for all concerned? Under those circumstances, he could have come to resent rather than love her—and their son.

"Dealing with an unintended pregnancy is very emotional. It's hard to think straight. I know I almost made the worst mistake of my life because of it."

Kristi's head snapped around. "You were in the same boat?"

"Hmm." Lizzie's eyes seemed to focus on some distant memory. "I was very much in love with Susie's biological father. He was exciting and fun to be with, something of an adventurer. He said he wanted one last fling before we got married, and he went off to the Amazon jungles in search of oil. After he left, I discovered I was pregnant.''

''And he didn't want to come back?''

''Actually, he tried. His plane crashed in the jungle.''

''Oh, Lizzie, I'm so sorry.''

''My parents were appalled that their beloved daughter—I was a former debutante, you see—was pregnant and unmarried. That simply wasn't acceptable in their social circle.''

''Phooey. It happens in the very best of families.''

''Mom! Mom!'' Adam shouted from inside the ring. ''Look at me!''

Her heart lurched when she saw String Bean had released the bridle and Adam was steering the horse on his own. She swallowed hard and forced a smile. ''Be careful, honey.''

''Me, too, Mommy!'' Nancy echoed, eager for her own moment of attention.

''I see you, sweetie.'' Lizzie waved at the tiny redhead. ''You're doing fine.'' In the backpack, Susie bounced up and down, telegraphing her own encouragement.

''The Tildens of San Francisco don't have babies out of wedlock,'' Lizzie said, as though two little children weren't risking life and limb on their respective horses. ''So my parents took it upon themselves to arrange a marriage for me to a politically ambitious man, whom they thought would be acceptable to their friends.''

"But not to you?" While Kristi's parents hadn't been thrilled with her pregnancy, they'd been more than supportive. She would always be grateful for that.

"I was so deep into grief, I was willing to agree to anything they said. Fortunately, both my mother and my groom-to-be wanted a big ceremony and didn't want a bride who was as big as a house. Too tacky, they said. So they all decided we'd wait until after Susie-Q was born."

From what Rory had told her, Kristi began to see a picture emerging. "You changed your mind."

"I almost waited until it was too late. I ran away about three days before the wedding and came here. Which, it turns out, was the smartest thing I'd ever done."

"My goodness, but you're courageous. A runaway bride and now a mother of five. That's quite a leap from debutante balls."

"Not only did I fall head over heels for Walker, I discovered motherhood is exactly right for me." Her satisfied smile, and the joy that sparkled in her clear blue eyes, spoke more loudly than her softly spoken words. "High society wasn't nearly as satisfying."

Susie stuck her thumb in her mouth and reached toward Kristi with her free hand.

Kristi responded with a nibble to the baby's fingers. She couldn't help but both admire and envy Lizzie. She'd found her place, the home where she belonged with the man and children she loved, here on the Double O. Kristi was still mired in confusion.

Except when she glanced across the corral, she

knew years ago she had found the man she would always love.

The home she'd dreamed about, the family she'd longed for, still eluded her.

Rory and Walker came sauntering around to their side of the corral. Rory was beaming with pride.

"Adam's a natural on a horse," he said.

"Which must mean he takes after his mother," Walker commented.

Rory whirled on his brother. "Hey, what do you mean by that? Didn't I win a medal at a junior rodeo and beat you in the process?"

"Yeah, *after* I taught you how to ride. Don't you remember the first time you got on a horse? You landed on your butt before we got out of the corral."

Rory shrugged indifferently. "How was I supposed to know it wasn't so easy to ride bareback. The Indians in the movies always managed."

"And you thought you were too smart to ride like a white man."

"So, I had an attitude problem. Like you and Eric weren't trying to lord it over me or anything—"

Lizzie caught Kristi's arm and led her away from the corral. "Those two can go on forever razzing each other about their boyhood pranks. Let's go fix some sandwiches. At least with their mouths full they won't pick on each other."

Kristi glanced over her shoulder. "But I don't like to leave Adam while—"

"He'll be fine. I promise."

Rationally, Kristi knew that was true. She also recognized the friendly kidding between Rory and

Walker was because they loved each other. They had a bond that wouldn't be easily broken.

Woe unto the person who tried.

Two DAYS LATER, Rory walked Adam across the road to Doc Justine's clinic. The boy had spent the afternoon with him as his "junior veterinarian's helper." It had been a kick to watch the youngster stack rolls of gauze and count cotton containers. There wasn't anything wrong with Adam's ability to stick to the job. And when Greg Vedor, an area rancher, brought in an injured bald eagle, Adam had been fascinated by the process of splinting the bird's wing. He'd barely breathed, he'd been so engaged in the procedure.

Near as Rory could tell, Adam's teacher wasn't challenging the boy enough. Boredom was the problem, not hyperactivity.

As they stepped into the entryway, Kristi was just walking a patient out of the clinic. Rory recognized the girl as Sherri Snodgrass, the oldest child of a big family that lived outside of town, the same family that had had to move into the shelter during the blizzard when the roof on their house collapsed. She wasn't older than sixteen and looked to be about six or seven months pregnant. She'd been crying, her eyes puffy.

Adam couldn't restrain his excitement. "Hey, Mom, guess what—"

"Just a minute, honey. I'm talking with a patient right now."

The boy snapped his mouth shut and bounced up

on his toes, though he didn't look happy about waiting his turn for his mother's attention. But he didn't argue. Kristi had on her nurse's game face accentuated by the turquoise medical jacket she wore and a stethoscope draped around her neck. White slacks and shoes rounded out the professional image.

She should have been a doctor, Rory reminded himself. Probably would have been if he hadn't gotten her pregnant.

"Be sure you take those vitamins, Sherri," Kristi reminded the girl as she reached the door. "And don't forget your next appointment. Doc Justine will come and get you if you don't show up."

The admonition was said kindly, but still the girl flushed. "I know. I'll get Dad to drive me into town again, even if he doesn't want to."

"Good." Kristi gave the girl's arm a squeeze. "Both you and your baby will be fine. I promise. You just have to take good care of yourself."

Still teary-eyed, the girl nodded and hustled out the door.

Practically jumping up and down by now, Adam blurted out his news. "Mom, I gots to be Dad's helper and I helped him to put a splint on an eagle's wing that got busted. Dad thinks he ran into a wire or something and that's how it got busted."

"My, that is exciting news." Kristi's eyes sparkled as she gave Adam a hug and smiled at Rory. "You're a lucky little boy."

"And Dad says tomorrow I gets to feed the bird, if I want. Did you know if a bird you catched and put in a cage starts eating, that means he's gonna be okay?''

"No, I guess I didn't know that."

"So I'm gonna feed him real, real carefully."

"I'm sure you—"

The boy wiggled out of Kristi's embrace. "I'm gonna go tell *both* grandmas. Bet they didn't know that, either." Boots clomping on the hardwood floor, he raced into the living room and through the swinging door on the other side that led into the kitchen.

Laughing, Kristi shook her head. "Evidently, Adam had a good time this afternoon."

"He's a great little kid. Smart as a whip."

Her smile faltered. "Yes, I know." She turned and walked back into the clinic.

Rory followed her. "I should be thanking you for doing such a good job raising Adam. You've done a terrific job."

She stopped to make some notes on the patient chart, then looked up. "I love him, Rory. I'd give my life for him without even thinking twice. The thought of losing him terrifies me."

"I understand." Worried that Kristi's love for Adam might keep him and his son apart, Rory shoved his hands in his jeans pockets. "That it for your patients today?"

"Yes. Justine's practice isn't exactly high pressure. Nothing like the clinic in Spokane. We had an infant with an ear infection earlier and a boy with a case of strep throat. One of the local ranchers has a bad ankle sprain." She wadded up the sheet she'd used during the examination and tossed it into a linen hamper.

"Sherri looked pretty upset when she left."

"Hmm." At the sink, she washed her hands with soap and dried them on a paper towel. "It isn't easy when you're sixteen and pregnant. She's mostly scared."

"Her boyfriend not around?"

"I don't think I'm revealing a confidence when I tell you he took off for parts unknown two days after she told him she was pregnant. Everyone in town seems to know about it, including her parents. It seems seventeen-year-old boys tend to be notoriously unreliable when it comes to paternity."

Rory experienced a stab of guilt. "I was a lot older than that, and I left you in the same fix."

"Not *that* much older." She folded her arms across her chest. Her hair was in slight disarray, her makeup faded at the end of the day. But despite that, to Rory she looked as beautiful as she had the first day he'd met her.

"I'm sorry, Kristi. God, I'm sorry. If I had known—"

"You would have tried to do the right thing."

"Yes." He'd failed her, and his throat ached with regret. "It had to be awful for you, being alone, I mean."

"I was lucky my parents were so supportive. But when I went into labor early…" She rubbed her hands up and down her arms as though the memory chilled her. "If Justine hadn't been there, I might have bled to death. Certainly losing the baby was a real possibility.''

One step forward and Rory gathered her into his arms. He'd seen the memory of fear in her eyes, the sense of desperation she'd experienced. He cursed himself for not being there for her, yet there was no way he could go back to change things.

Relaxing against him, she rested her head on his shoulder. He inhaled deeply of the scent of her apple shampoo. The sweet fragrance taunted him. Made him want her with a fierceness that almost frightened him, and he pulled her more tightly into his embrace.

The urge to do more than hold Kristi burrowed into his awareness. A medical examining room, with their son and Kristi's mother and grandmother only two rooms away, was not the time or place to give in to the hunger that gnawed at his belly, demanding to be satisfied.

He hadn't made love to her since the cabin. He'd been too shocked, too angry with her, after he discovered he had a son to think of anything except her betrayal.

But the desire was back, more potent than before because the memories of holding her, loving her, were more recent. He knew how it would feel to slide into her heat, be enveloped by her moist glove. Feel her clench around him and come apart in his arms.

He stifled the moan that threatened.

If they couldn't go back, could they go forward together? He and Kristi and their son?

Behind him, he heard Kristi's mother discreetly clearing her throat.

Reluctantly, he released Kristi. She stepped away, leaving him with a painful sense of loss. How could he let her go again? How could he keep her here in Grass Valley, away from the life she'd chosen?

"Sorry to interrupt," Dottie said. "I've fixed pot roast tonight. We hope you'll stay for supper, Rory."

When he checked with Kristi, she gave an almost imperceptible nod of approval. She seemed shaken, as affected by their embrace as he had been. That had to mean they could work things out, he reasoned. He just didn't know how.

To her mother he said, "I'd be happy to stay, Mrs. Kerrigan. A home-cooked meal is always a treat for me."

The older woman eyed him and Kristi, and smiled. "I think you can call me Dottie. Or Grandma like Adam does, if that's easier."

Heat rushed to Rory's cheeks. He'd never in his life called anyone grandma. He'd barely known his own mother much less any relatives. And he had never been caught holding anybody's daughter, particularly when the evidence of his arousal was so apparent.

"Yes, ma'am. I'll, uh, just go wash up."

Chapter Twelve

"And Dad says he's gonna get me some books on wolves and eagles and stuff, and then I'm gonna read 'em and be a vet just like him."

The two grandmothers at the dinner table made suitably appropriate responses to Adam's excited ramblings.

"That's wonderful, dear," Dottie said, her smile encouraging. "I'm sure you'll be wonderful at anything you want to do."

Justine, who sat at the head of the table with her leg propped on a footstool, said, "You sure you want to work with all those smelly creatures? You could be a *real* doctor, you know."

"A vet's an *animal* doctor, Grandma Justy. You gotta be *real* smart to do that."

It was just as well Dottie and Justine were able to carry on a conversation with Adam. Kristi's thought processes had been totally jumbled since Rory had held her in the examining room. Her body had reacted forcefully, too. Every nerve ending had tingled in anticipation of more than his embrace. Every feminine atom had quickened. Desire had surged through her as though someone had administered an IV filled with concentrated hormones directly into her bloodstream.

Those same chemicals were still flooding through her body nearly an hour later.

Ignoring the serving of roast beef and potatoes on her plate, she glanced across the table at Rory. A proud smile teased around the corners of his sensual lips as he listened to his son chatter on about the merits of becoming a veterinarian.

What Kristi wanted was to feel Rory's lips on hers again. Wanted his firm yet gentle insistence that she respond to him. The stroke of his tongue parting her lips. The press of his chest against her breasts. The soaring sensation that only he could bring her with little more than a kiss.

He looked in her direction, and she felt heat steal up from her midsection to stain her cheeks. A pulse ticked rapidly in her throat, echoed by a throbbing much lower in her body.

How was it possible after so many years of abstaining from intimate encounters that her all-too-brief interlude with Rory at the cabin had reawakened her dormant sexual desire? Literally overnight she'd become addicted to his kisses, to the way he made love to her. And like an addict, going cold-turkey without her drug of choice caused her physical pain. She'd sweated every night since their return to Grass Valley. But even her erotic dreams couldn't measure up to the reality of what she'd experienced in his arms.

He cocked a brow as though he knew what she was thinking. Feeling. And his slow smile broadened, crinkling the corners of his dark eyes. "Guess I'd better start putting money away for college tuition for him, huh?"

She licked her lips and swallowed against the dryness in her throat. "That assumes Miss Zidbeck will recommend him for regular kindergarten and he survives the rest of elementary school."

"He'll manage, probably a lot better than his old man did."

Rory wasn't old. *Potent* came to mind. *Virile* and *compelling*. His mere presence an overdose to her good reason.

"How about you come to the next teacher conference?" she suggested, forcing herself to keep the conversation light. "Miss Zidbeck would be happy to discuss Adam's progress with you."

"It would be a long drive, but I'll be there. Just let me know when and where."

His reference to the distance they lived apart sliced through her like a knife, and her heart bled at the pain.

Her mother heard Rory's remark. "Whenever you're in Spokane, you plan to stay with us, all right? We've plenty of room."

"If you come to Spokane," Adam said, "you could meet Troy. Then he'd know I wasn't lying 'bout having a dad 'n' being an Indian and stuff. You'd show him."

Rory rested his hand on the back of the boy's head and ruffled his hair. "Yeah, I would. Speaking of which, I want to call a friend of mine, a Blackfeet tribal leader.'' He glanced toward Kristi, his gaze turning serious. ''Before you leave, I'd like to arrange a naming ceremony for Adam. Being Indian is an important part of his ancestry.''

Before you leave.

For a moment, Kristi couldn't breathe. If she hadn't been trained as a nurse, she would have been convinced her heart had stopped dead in her chest. Maybe it had.

''Naming ceremony?'' Her voice rose barely above a whisper.

''It's like a baptism except it's a lot more fun,'' Grandma Justine explained. ''Drums. Dancing. The whole tribe hops around honoring whomever is being named. It can be quite a party.''

''Do I gets an Indian name?'' The boy's dark eyes, so like his father's, sparked with excitement.

''Sure, that's the whole idea,'' Rory said. ''That way you'll always be part of the tribe just like me.''

''Wow! Can I be chief someday?''

Everyone chuckled except Kristi. Her heart was in her throat. Minute by minute she felt Adam slipping away from her, becoming more his father's son than hers. She tried not to resent that. Rory had already missed too much of his son's life. But she didn't want to miss the rest.

''There might be a few other men in line ahead of you, but maybe someday.'' Rory glanced at Justine. ''I'm hoping you'll help me out with ideas for the giveaway.''

''What's a giveaway?'' Adam wanted to know.

"It's a tribal custom. The person being honored gives presents to the members of the tribe."

"You mean it's *my* party and I gotta give away all the stuff to *them?*"

The boy looked so appalled, Kristi laughed with everyone else. Apparently there was still some merit in the traditions Adam had grown up with.

Rory made it clear they were all invited to the naming ceremony. It would be a family affair.

"I'll come," Justine said grumpily. "But you won't catch me prancing and dancing around on my crutches. I'll leave that up to you young folks."

For Kristi, curiosity mingled with an uneasy feeling she'd be out of place at a tribal ceremony. But for Adam's sake she needed to have some understanding of that part of his ancestry. Maybe she needed that for herself, too, because it was important to the man she loved.

As Rory left Justine's place after dinner and headed across the road to his home, he was struck by how *normal* it had felt to be sitting at the dinner table with Adam, Kristi and her mother. Even Doc Justine's acerbic tongue didn't have the sharp edge it sometimes had.

His thoughts drifted back to the years he'd spent growing up on the Double O. Since Oliver Oakes had been a widower, there'd never been a woman at the table there. No one to soften the unruly manners of three adolescent boys. Left to their own devices, he and his brothers had roughhoused their way through meals, poking and jabbing at each other until Oliver had been forced to settle them down. He'd probably been more patient than a woman would have been under the same circumstances.

Rory and his brothers had grown up without much experience with the gentler side of life.

Rory found he liked Kristi's quiet voice, the way she spoke to his son. Her calming influence over the boy.

Not that her unruffled behavior calmed Rory down one iota. He'd been edgy all evening, thinking about how much he wanted to make love to her again. It had been damn hard to keep his head in the conversation and talk about Adam's naming ceremony when what Rory really wanted was to drag Kristi back to the examining room to finish what they'd barely started with her in his arms.

By the next morning, when the phone woke him before dawn, he realized he wouldn't have a chance to finish anything soon.

After listening to the foreman of the Bar X Ranch, a big spread in the neighboring county, explain his problem, Rory said, "I'll be there as soon as I can, Floyd."

Hanging up, he sat groggily on the edge of the bed and ran his fingers through his hair. Normally if he was called away for a day or two he'd ask Eric to fill in for him, caring for any animals he might have in his kennel for treatment. He could do that now.

Or he could ask Kristi. Maybe if she knew a little more about his veterinary practice...

Picking up the phone again, he punched in Doc Justine's number. After one ring he heard Kristi's sleepy voice.

"Doctor's office."

He pictured her strawberry-blond hair all sleep mussed, her skin soft and warm from the bed, and his body stirred at the thought. "Kristi, it's me. Rory."

"What's wrong?" Her tone was alert now, wide-awake and filled with concern.

"Nothing's wrong, at least not with me." Except for the painful arousal that he'd felt the moment he heard her voice. "I'm going to have to be away for a couple of days. The Bar X Ranch in Hill County has a couple of cows in trouble trying to drop their calves."

"Oh." Silence hummed over the phone line for a moment. "Adam will miss you."

"Yeah, I'll miss him, too." *And you.* "I was thinking maybe you and he could feed the wolf and the eagle for me. Adam knows what to do, and I'll leave written instructions just in case he gets confused."

"I'm sure he'd be tickled to do that."

"It won't be a pain for you? I mean, you've got Doc's patients to worry about."

"No, it's fine. Except for food and water, the animals pretty well take care of themselves, don't they?"

"That's right." He wanted to linger on the phone with her, listen a little longer to her melodic voice. "The thing is, this might be a good chance for me. I've heard that the vet in Shelby the Bar X normally uses is planning to retire soon. If they like my work and start calling me, well, that could mean some whopping big fees down the road.'' He'd be able to pay down his debts in a hurry.

''Then you have to go,'' she agreed.

''Well, if you're okay with kennel-sitting, I'd better get my gear together. Thanks.''

''No problem.''

He was about to hang up when he heard her whisper in a seductive, sultry voice, ''Drive carefully and come home safe.''

''I will.''

''We'll be waiting for you.''

Smiling to himself, he cradled the phone. He hoped the cows at the Bar X dropped their calves in a hurry because he was already anxious to get back home.

Never before had any woman been waiting for his return.

FOR THE PAST TWO DAYS, Kristi had felt at loose ends. She and Adam had faithfully fed the wild creatures in their care, her son virtually strutting with pride at having been given such a grown-up responsibility. Meanwhile, she'd handled the human patients who had shown up at Grandma Justine's clinic.

But mostly Kristi had found herself at odd moments gazing out the window at Rory's house. Missing him. Hoping she'd see his truck drive up. Wishing he were there. She marveled that she could miss him so much after only two days when she'd managed to survive for almost six long years without seeing him at all.

Just after supper he'd called to say he was on the way. He'd sounded eager. So was she. Foolishly so.

After getting Adam to bed, she'd paced around Doc's clinic, fussing with the medical supplies, straightening the exam rooms about ten times more than they needed to be touched. Glancing out the window.

The wait had been all the more difficult after the call from the Spokane clinic that morning. Soon she'd have to leave Grass Valley. They needed her back at work.

Finally she'd given in to her urge to check that she'd left everything in order at Rory's place.

She swiped at the top of his stove one last time. The kitchen sparkled. She'd even cleaned out his refrigerator, a task she generally loathed. Not that Rory had much in his refrigerator except butter and eggs and a half can of molding chili con carne. She didn't really need to be here. He'd probably be tired when he got home. There'd be plenty of opportunity to see him tomorrow.

Headlights flicked across the kitchen windows. Her heart lurched.

Impulsively she hurried to the door and pulled it open. She had just enough time to see his surprise and pleasure before he swept her into his arms. His jacket was cold from the night air, his whiskers dark and unshaven, his eyes rimmed with fatigue. Yet suddenly she felt warmer than she had in the past two days.

"You're home safe."

"I'm here. And you feel good."

"You must be exhausted."

"I'm not too tired for this." His mouth closed over hers in a bruising kiss that reached clear to her soul with its determined demand for a response.

She gave him what he asked for. Opening for him, she wrapped her arms around his middle beneath his jacket and angled her head to give him better access to her mouth. He tasted of rich, black coffee and robust masculinity. She rubbed her hands over the broad expanse of his back, and muscles grew taut beneath her palms.

He speared his fingers through her hair, capturing her as surely as a snare captured a wild creature. She couldn't move. Didn't want to. She wouldn't struggle against the prison of his arms, the lure of his mouth, the intertwining of their tongues. In this moment in time, she belonged here. With him.

She trembled at the coiling tightness that rose in her. The sense of *rightness.* How could two people stay apart when they were meant to be together?

With a low, throaty groan, his mouth left hers and found the tender column of her neck. He nipped beneath her ear, his teeth gentle, then soothed her with his tongue. Gooseflesh raced down her spine only to meet the rising heat from her belly.

"Rory?" she gasped.

"I want you." The words, his voice, held an edge of desperation.

She was desperate, too. "Yes. Please." She shoved his jacket off his shoulders.

He lifted her sweater over her head, all the time walking her backward toward his bedroom and kissing her lips, her eyes, her forehead. The double bed was there. She'd made it neatly with clean sheets the day he left. With a single sweep of his hand, he sent the covers flying. The commanding, erotic gesture inflamed her. Made her tremble. Tonight would not be filled with gentle love but the passionate sort that would leave them both breathless.

He shoved her jeans down below her hips. She undid his belt but couldn't get the snaps on his fly to release. With a low, feral snarl he did it himself, and he burst free.

She toed her shoes off, then shimmied out of her jeans. Somehow he rid himself of his boots. And they tumbled onto the bed, rolling and touching and kissing.

Sobbing, she made little cries of wanting and need. She was barely aware of him removing her panties, catching the clasp of her bra and tossing it aside while she did the same for his shirt. His jeans were gone before she realized he'd discarded them.

He caressed and stroked, murmuring sweet words that both soothed and stoked the fires that were raging inside her. She begged for more as he spread her knees apart. And then there was nothing but spiraling sensation. Hot and wanton. A total vulnerability that she had never before known. An opening of herself, a giving until she had nothing left to give.

With a final thrust, he sent her mindlessly into some other time and space. She soared. Felt him follow her. And then, contractions still pulsing through her, she slowly returned to earth, her muscles limp, her body boneless.

Above her, Rory's eyes were dark and sensual, filled with mastery before he collapsed his weight onto her. She sighed with pleasure, relishing the sensation of their joining. How well they fit together. As though they were always meant to be as one.

Time moved in slow motion with an ethereal quality. She floated on mental clouds that had her drifting in and out of the here and now. She might have slept. Or perhaps not, though she couldn't remember Rory rolling off her and gathering her in his arms. But that's where she found herself, her head resting on his shoulder, his arms around her. His chest lifted with each even breath.

"Rory?"

"Hmm." His slow breathing didn't miss a beat.

"The Spokane clinic called this morning. They wanted to be sure I was coming back to work next week. The other nurse practitioner's mother is ill and she needs to take some time off."

"Hmm." He nuzzled his face into the crook of her neck, his breath hot on her bare flesh.

Had he heard her? She couldn't be sure. After the way they'd made love, she'd hoped he would ask her to stay in Grass Valley. Had prayed he'd ask her to marry him.

But years ago she'd had the same dream.

Dreams, she had learned, don't always come true. Even recurring dreams.

Carefully she eased herself out of Rory's embrace. He muttered something unintelligible and rolled over, his sleep undisturbed. Somehow, after all these years, she hadn't managed to touch his heart.

Biting back the tears that threatened, she found her clothes, dressed and slipped back into Grandma Justine's house under cover of darkness. No one would know how foolish she'd been—again.

Only she would know that in these two weeks in Grass Valley she had lost her heart for a second time.

Rory lay stock-still until he heard the door closing behind her. *She was going back to Spokane.* The clinic needed her.

So did he, but where would he ever find the guts to ask her to stay?

As a kid, he'd searched for the reason his mom had deserted him. Oliver Oakes had tried to convince Rory it wasn't his fault. Rory knew that wasn't the truth.

At some elemental level, he wasn't lovable enough that his mother had wanted to keep him.

More than twenty years later things hadn't changed much.

THE NEXT MORNING at the clinic, Kristi saw two more strep throats, an ear infection and took a blood sample to check Hetty Moore's cholesterol level, which she would send off to a lab in Great Falls later in the day.

Then she did a pap smear for a rancher's wife from the next county.

"I've surely been glad to have Doc Justine all these years," Iona Gaffey said as she sat up on the examination table. "I just don't like a man doctor poking around down there."

Kristi pulled off her gloves and smiled at her patient. "Trust me, man or woman, the only thing a doctor is interested in is seeing healthy pink tissue."

"I know that. Still, I feel lots more comfortable with a woman, if you know what I mean."

Kristi understood, and over the years of dealing with doctors of both sexes, she generally preferred a woman doctor, as well.

"Anything else bothering you, Mrs. Gaffey?" Kristi also knew women were more likely to open up to another woman than a man. "Any unusual bleeding? Fatigue?"

She laughed. "Doctor, I'm a rancher's wife with five kids, most of 'em teenagers. Being tired comes with the territory."

Kristi didn't bother to correct the misunderstanding about her being a doctor. She had only a few days left in Grass Valley, anyway. "I want you to be sure to get an appointment for your mammogram in Great Falls. According to your chart, it's time."

"Oh, I know that. As soon as I'm sure we won't get another snowfall, I'll make an appointment. The kids and I will make a day of it, do a little shopping."

"Good for you." Kristi rested her hand lightly on the woman's shoulder. She'd never questioned that touch had the power to heal or at least encourage confidences. "Anything else, you let me or Doc Justine know, okay?"

"I'll do that. Doc Justine's been a good friend to us all for a lot of years. It's too bad about her ankle."

Kristi left the examining room so the woman could dress. In the small cubicle Grandma Justine called her office, Kristi made notes on Mrs. Gaffey's chart and filled out the forms to ship the tissue sample to the lab. She heard Mrs. Gaffey leave and had just finished her paperwork when Justine hobbled into the room on her crutches.

She sat down in the chair opposite Kristi. "My patients seemed to have developed a lot of confidence in you, young lady."

Kristi laid down her pen. "I'm sure it's only because they know you're only steps away if I need you."

"Nonsense. They recognize competence when they see it. You're good, young lady. You always have been."

She flushed at her grandmother's praise. "I had a good role model."

"Humph." She fussed with the gold pen-and-pencil desk set with a marble base that had been inscribed in her honor by the townspeople of Grass Valley ten years ago. "It's been good to have you here, child. I always dreamed of you taking over my practice someday."

As an adolescent, so had Kristi. But that wasn't likely to happen since she was a nurse practitioner not an M.D.

"I've enjoyed being here, Grandma."

"I suspect that's as much because of the young man who lives across the street as me. I heard you come in late last night."

Kristi couldn't meet her gaze.

"Don't be ashamed. I haven't forgotten for a minute what it was like to fall in love with your grandpa, the ol' coot. He wasn't supposed to go off and leave me so early, either. And let me tell you, when I get past those pearly gates, he's gonna hear about that.''

In spite of herself, Kristi smiled. ''I'm sure he will, Grandma.''

''Now, tell me.'' She leaned forward. ''You and that young man across the road work out your differences?''

''Not really. I know Rory wants to be involved in Adam's life—''

''I'm not talking about the boy. I'm talking about the two of you.''

Pursing her lips together, Kristi shook her head. Rory knew she was needed back in Spokane. He hadn't asked her to stay. Perhaps that said it all.

Justine leaned back and rubbed her hand across her thigh as though the muscles were aching. ''I had a really interesting chat with Dr. Thaddeus Jones from Great Falls a couple of weeks ago. He's one of those hotsie-totsie doctors, a board-certified internist. Used to be we'd call him a general practitioner, but that's not good enough for 'em anymore. All those young doctors are more interested in getting initials after their names instead of experience.''

Kristi wasn't sure where this conversation was going so she waited silently and watched her grandmother struggle to get to the point.

''I've been thinking of retiring, you know?''

She almost gasped in surprise. Somehow the image of her grandmother retired simply wouldn't form. She was too vital, too energetic. Too opinionated to watch the world go by without making her own contribution to society.

"Doc Jones is thinking about expanding his practice, buying up smaller clinics that aren't exactly self-supporting and running them on a part-time basis with nurse practitioners in charge of the day-to-day stuff. He'd have office hours at the clinics one or two days a week and be on call the rest of the time. He claims it's a cost-effective way to run a medical practice."

The possibilities spun through Kristi's head in a whirlwind. She hadn't considered… The possibility hadn't crossed her mind until… What would Rory say? Could she stay in Grass Valley knowing Rory was across the road yet not be a part of his life? What would be best for her son?

Her vision blurred and pain throbbed at her temple. Without Rory's love, how could she see him every day and survive her broken heart?

Vaguely she became aware of the next patient arriving and taking a seat outside the door to wait for her.

She forced herself to speak. "You're considering Dr. Jones's offer?" The words caught in her throat on both fear and hope.

Using her crutches, Justine levered herself to her feet. "I might. *If* I could find the right nurse practitioner willing to take on the job. Or maybe I might hire one myself and settle for being semiretired. You interested?"

"I'll have to think about it, Grandma." Long and hard. Too much was at stake to make the decision without considering all of the ramifications.

Including the ability of her heart to withstand the

stress of seeing Rory every day without being allowed to love him.

It was a decision she'd have to make on her own without the undue influence of passion. That meant in the few days remaining to her in Grass Valley, she'd have to keep her distance from Rory.

Her legs trembled as she got up to greet her next patient. Staying away from Rory, not succumbing to the urge to repeat the sensual hours they'd shared last night, might be the most difficult thing she'd ever done in her life.

Chapter Thirteen

The morning of the naming ceremony dawned bright and clear, the sky a Wedgwood blue. Except in shady spots, the snow had melted, and the fields were tinted fluorescent green with new shoots of grass. As though excited by the arrival of spring, redwing blackbirds and flocks of tiny brown sparrows darted from bush to fence post and back again, perching only briefly on the telephone lines that stretched toward the horizon.

Kristi sat in the front seat of Rory's SUV. Adam was in the back along with Grandma Justine and Kristi's mother. Behind them were cartons of presents for members of the Blackfeet tribe.

"Are we almost there?" Adam asked for about the twentieth time in the past two hours.

"Soon." Rory glanced into the rearview mirror and smiled. "Browning is right up ahead. The school where they're holding the powwow is near the middle of town."

Rory looked every inch the Indian in buckskin leggings and a matching shirt decorated with porcupine quills and painted symbols, the open collar providing a glimpse of his tanned throat. His moccasins were made of deerskin with soft leather soles.

Kristi could easily imagine him riding across the prairie on an Indian pony instead of being behind the wheel of an SUV. In either case, he'd be the most handsome man for miles around.

Adam wore a shirt similar to Rory's and had strutted around the house to show it off last night when Rory brought it over. It had taken all of Kristi's parenting skills to prevent the boy from sleeping in the shirt without bringing on a full-fledged tantrum. Finally they'd compromised, hanging the garment on a chair near Adam's bed where he could put it on first thing this morning.

Kristi was less confident she was appropriately dressed. A broom skirt and matching blouse she'd purchased at the general store was the best she could find.

The two grandmothers in the back seat had chosen casual dresses to wear.

"Are there gonna be tomtoms?" Mimicking the sound of a drum, Adam slapped his thighs.

"There'll be drums when we dance."

"Will I get to play 'em?"

"Not for the dancing part. You have to lead that."

"I've never danced before."

"It's easy. All you have to do is lead us around in a circle."

Adam's smooth forehead furrowed into a frown of concentration. "I remember. It's like follow-the-leader."

"Pretty much."

"Will I get to go 'ooo-ooo-ooo'?" He patted his mouth as he formed a childish Indian war whoop.

Rory's lips twitched with the threat of another smile. "That probably won't be necessary." He slowed the truck as they entered the city limits.

Browning looked to be a typical western town with a scruffy main street lined with equally scruffy cars and trucks parked in front of aging buildings that housed various commercial establishments. Pedestrians ambled along the sidewalks or jaywalked across the street, intent on completing their Saturday errands. Small as Browning was, Grass Valley was only half the size, and it felt to Kristi as though she were on an outing to the big city.

The high school was quite modern, the parking lot filled with dozens of the same vintage trucks she'd seen on the main street. Every vehicle was spattered with mud from traveling the dirt roads that fanned out through the reservation.

Rory parked at the end of a row of cars and trucks and switched off the ignition. Almost before his feet touched the ground, Adam had scrambled over the console and out of the truck.

"Whoa, slow down, son." He snared the boy by the arm. "We've gotta wait for your grandma Justy. She can't move as fast as she used to."

"You got that right," she grumbled.

Rory took her crutches from her and helped Justine out of the truck. "We have to carry in all the presents, too, champ. It wouldn't be much of a giveaway without them."

"Isn't *anybody* going to give me a present?"

Kristi came around the end of the truck and gave her son a squeeze. "How about a nice motherly hug? Won't that do?" Adam's responding scowl made her laugh.

On the school field adjacent to the parking lot, several youngsters were engaged in a pickup game of soccer, yelling encouragement to their teammates.

From the back of the truck, Rory handed her a carton of crayons and coloring books that they would give to the younger children. For the older boys there were small model airplanes; the girls were to receive hair decorations. There were earrings for the women, flashlights that snapped onto dashboards for the men. The elders were to receive lush Pendleton blankets. And for his friend and tribal leader, Jimmy Deer Running, Rory had selected a leather jacket.

Everyone except Grandma Justine carried something into the gymnasium. Despite her crutches, she was getting around much better now than when Kristi had brought her home from the hospital. In another few weeks the cast would come off and Justine would be back to normal.

And ready to retire from active medical practice.

Kristi's anxiety rose a notch when she stepped into the huge room.

A hundred people milled about on the gym floor between the two basketball hoops or sat clustered together in the spectator stands. Many of them were dressed in traditional Indian garb similar to what Rory wore, the women in beautifully decorated long dresses, the men in leggings. Others were dressed in contemporary clothing, jeans or skirts and tops.

And everywhere she looked she saw dark-haired, dark-eyed people, all of them resembling Rory—and her son. With her reddish-blond hair and blue eyes, she felt out of place. An interloper who had no business crashing their party.

"Wow, Mom! Look at him," her son cried.

She followed his gaze to a man in full Indian regalia including a feather headdress composed of eagle feathers that hung down his back almost to the floor. His face was weather worn, and he carried himself regally, an imposing figure of a man.

"Jimmy Deer Running." Rory set the box down he was carrying, and the two men clasped forearms, embraced and clapped each other's back.

"*Oki,*" Jimmy said in greeting. "It is a long time between your visits to Browning."

"Winter travel isn't easy."

"For any of us, which is why everyone was pleased to come together for a naming ceremony today." His gaze lowered to Adam. "And this is the young man who seeks to be a part of the Blackfeet nation?"

Adam's eyes were round with excitement. "Wow! Are you really a chief?"

Jimmy chuckled. "Yes, I am the Old One."

Rory made introductions. "Jimmy Deer Running, this is my son, Adam, his mother Kristi Kerrigan, her mother, Dottie Kerrigan. You probably know Doc Justine."

"I do." He had a special smile for Justine, then

acknowledged Kristi and her mother. "Welcome to you all. We are always pleased to have guests at our ceremonies."

"Thank you," Kristi murmured in unison with her mother.

"You keeping your grandkids out of hornets' nests these days, Jimmy?" Justine asked, apparently referring to an incident in the past.

"Doing my best, Doctor. But these days young people do not always listen to their elders."

"We've got the same problem over in Grass Valley." Justine gave Kristi an accusing look, which she ignored.

Grandma Justine might want her to stay in town to work with her or the new doctor but that wasn't an easy decision to make. Not unless Rory extended a far more personal invitation, which hadn't been forthcoming. Kristi had about given up hope. She planned to leave tomorrow in order to be at work Monday morning.

Other friends of Rory's appeared to say hello, and introductions were made. Everyone seemed friendly and did their best to make Kristi feel at home, which didn't entirely ease her anxiety. This was Rory's world, these his people. She would never truly belong here.

She was smiling politely at one of his Indian friends when she looked up to see Walker, Lizzie and their clan of adolescents and babies walk in the gym door.

"I didn't expect to see you here," she said to Walker.

"These things are family affairs. Bird Brain is definitely part of the family." He and Rory did a brotherly version of an affectionate hug, which looked a lot like a wrestling hold.

Moments later Eric appeared, and the process was repeated.

Finally, when everyone seemed present and most were seated in the stands, Jimmy Deer Running called Adam to join him, gesturing that both Kristi and Rory should come, too.

"I won't know what to do," she whispered to Rory.

"Don't worry. You won't have to say or do anything, just be there for Adam."

Glancing around self-consciously, she walked onto the gym floor with Rory and Adam. The boy stood on a handwoven blanket that Jimmy had placed on the floor, Rory and Kristi standing behind him. Adam's eyes glowed with excitement, and his cheeks were flushed, but he didn't fidget. Instead, he solemnly watched the proceedings, never taking his eyes from Jimmy and his regalia of feathers and decorated buckskin.

In a firm, sonorous voice, Jimmy began speaking in the Blackfeet language. Kristi couldn't understand the details, but it was obvious that everyone took the ceremony seriously. This was an important moment in her son's life, and pride welled in her chest. Adam was now as much a member of the Blackfeet tribe as Rory was.

Only she remained an outsider.

"And now your name," Jimmy said in clear English. "From this day forward you will be known among our people as Adam Little Gray Wolf."

With a gentle smile, the chief eased Adam off the blanket. Rory picked it up, wrapping it around his son's shoulders and hugged the boy.

To Kristi's surprise, tears dampened her cheeks as musicians began to beat out a rhythm on their skin-covered drums. Those who had been watching from the stands came down to the gym floor, the women draping shawls around their shoulders. Men, women and children all shook hands with Adam, welcoming him into the tribe.

She was still trying to blink the tears away when Rory took her hand.

"It's time for Adam to lead us in the honoring dance."

"But I don't know how to—"

"You'll get the hang of it in no time." He waved for Kristi's mother to come, too.

"Does Adam know how to do this dance?" she asked.

"Dad 'n' me have been practicing," Adam said proudly, clinging to the blanket draped around his slender shoulders like a talisman.

"Did you hear, Mom? I'm Adam Little Gray Wolf now?"

Bending, she kissed him. "Yes, I heard. I love you, son."

"Yeah, me, too, Mom. Can we dance now, Dad? Can we?"

"You bet, son."

Everyone flowed into a line behind Adam: Kristi

and Rory side by side behind him, followed by Kristi's mother and some of the tribal members. They all began to dance, swaying up and down with great dignity in rhythm to the music.

All of the Oakes family joined in the line, the teen-age boys particularly self-conscious even as they surveyed the adolescent girls scattered throughout the crowd.

By keeping an eye on the other dancers, Kristi was able to follow the steps. The rhythm wasn't complicated, the movements simple, but she felt the swirl of pride emanating from the participants. This was a celebration not only of Adam's naming but of their own ancestry. Kristi found she was proud to have some small part in their ceremony.

After the dancing came the time for the giveaways. Kristi helped distribute the presents and discovered the children were almost as excited to get a small present as Adam had been to receive his Indian name. It was like Christmas in April. The youngsters couldn't have been happier.

And Adam couldn't have been more thrilled to have his largesse so well received. Perhaps the lesson learned was that it was just as much fun to give as to receive.

Eventually the excitement slowed down. Feeling uneasy and uncertain of the future, Kristi walked out of the gym and took a deep breath of clear, refreshing air. To the west, the peaks of Glacier National Park were still capped with snow. She stood for a moment watching as the sun dropped behind them, casting the mountains in shadow.

In the same way, she felt a shadow had fallen over her and the life she'd built for herself. In the brief span of two weeks her whole life had changed—and so had her son's. He had a father now.

Would he still want or need a mother?

FOLLOWING all the excitement of the giveaway, Rory looked around for Kristi and couldn't spot her. Her mother was sitting with Doc Justine in the stands. His brothers had left, claiming ranch chores needed to be done. Adam was playing with some of his new friends, tossing the lightweight model airplanes around the gym.

But no Kristi.

Chills of panic grazed the back of his neck. Where could she have gone?

He headed for the door, avoided a collision with a toddler who was escaping from his mother and stepped outside. He squinted in the bright sunlight, quickly scanning the playing field. When he saw Kristi, he exhaled in relief.

She was standing alone, hugging herself in the cooling afternoon air as she gazed toward the mountains. The sun painted red and gold highlights in her hair. A gentle breeze fluttered her skirt, brushing the hem against her ankles. She looked beautiful, vulnerable and troubled.

Rory had an urge to take her in his arms, protect her from whatever was bothering her. He hadn't been there for her when she discovered she was pregnant. Hadn't helped her raise their son. In doing it on her own, she'd proved she didn't need him.

Despair stole the warmth from his soul. What if *he* needed *her?*

He approached quietly. "Checking out the scenery?" The tightness in his throat made his voice scratchy.

"Hmm." She turned to look up at him. Her cheeks were pale, her eyes troubled. She glanced past him toward the gym. "Where's Adam?"

"Playing airplane dogfights with the other boys. He's okay."

Her lower lip trembled. "I'm afraid I'm losing him."

"Losing Adam? Why would you think—"

"Living in a suburb can't compete with all of this." She made a vague gesture that included the mountains, the schoolyard and beyond. "I can't compete with being an Indian or letting a little boy fix an eagle's broken wing or having a wolf in my backyard. I'm just a single mother trying to juggle my job and look after my son. I have to discipline him. Make him take his baths. Do his homework. I'm not *you.* I'm not his father."

He palmed her cheek, thumbing off a tear that had fallen. "This isn't a competition, Kristi. Adam needs both a mother and father, and now he has that."

"So we shuttle him back and forth when it suits our respective schedules?"

No, that wasn't want he wanted. But he was afraid to ask. Afraid he didn't deserve the happiness he'd always dreamed about. He'd failed her once. How could he be sure he wouldn't fail again?

"We'll work it out somehow. Other parents do."

Another tear edged down her cheek, and he wiped it away. His tears were lodged in his throat.

She pursed her lips to prevent another tremor. "I have to leave tomorrow so I can be at work Monday morning. I have to take Adam with me. He can't miss any more school."

"I understand." The kids in Grass Valley went to school. There was even a prekindergarten class. Adam could go, too. Hell, the school was less than a quarter mile from his house. But that didn't appear to be a choice. "The injured wolf is well enough to take back to where we found him. I think Adam would like to be in on the release. We could do it tomorrow morning. Before you leave."

Slowly, she nodded. "Yes, he'd like that."

Tomorrow he would open a cage door and the wolf would be gone. So would Kristi and their son.

It wasn't right to keep either an animal or a person imprisoned against their will.

If Kristi wanted to stay in Grass Valley, she'd be the one to make that decision. Rory couldn't force her.

BY BEDTIME Adam was whiny with fatigue, exhausted from all of the day's excitement. His suitcase stood open on top of a small bookcase in the bedroom corner, his clothes already packed. The toys he'd brought from home had been crammed into his backpack for the ride to Spokane. Only his ceremonial shirt had yet to be put away. Kristi would do that in the morning, the last item to be packed.

"But *why* can't Dad come home with us?" Adam complained.

Kristi sat down on the bed beside him. "We've talked about this before, honey. Your father works here in Grass Valley. He can't simply leave his veterinary practice."

"But why not? He could get a job in Spokane, couldn't he?"

"I don't know." She smoothed back his hair from his forehead, the raven strands as wayward as his father's.

"Then why don't you get a job here? You could work for Grandma Justy. She'd let you."

"I don't think that would work out very well." Kristi imagined the pain of seeing Rory every day without being able to love him. The thought was unbearable.

"But *why-y-y?*" He dragged the word into two long, frustrated syllables that snapped Kristi's patience.

"Young man, it's past time for you to be asleep. If you want to help Rory with the wolf's release tomorrow then you'd better settle down right now."

"Me 'n' the wolf are brothers." Puffing his lips into a pout, he flipped over onto his side. "Dad'll let me go no matter what you say."

"Don't count on it, honey bunch." Leaning over, she brushed a kiss to his temple and tucked the blankets under his chin. "Sleep tight."

So far she and Rory hadn't crossed swords over disciplining Adam. They'd been on something of a honeymoon as a family, however tentative that relationship might be.

But living several hundred miles apart with both her and Rory involved in raising their son could change that—very likely for the worse.

RORY JAMMED HIS HANDS in his jacket pockets.

After eating dinner with Kristi and her family and telling Adam good-night, he'd come back to his place to get everything ready to transport the wolf back to the area of the Durfee cabin tomorrow. He'd fed the injured eagle. He'd tried to watch TV, but there wasn't anything on worth seeing. It was too early to go to bed, and he wasn't likely to sleep anyway.

He was too darn restless and edgy with wanting.

Glancing across the road, he noted the light was still on in Kristi's room but the rest of the house was dark. She was probably packing to leave.

God, he'd miss her.

Whirling, he marched toward Main Street. Everything was closed up tight except the saloon. Tinny music and raucous laughter drifted out through the windows. He didn't want a drink. And he sure didn't want to talk to a bunch of Saturday-night cowboys.

Instead he arrowed past the sheriff's office toward the two-story house on a couple of acres where his brother lived. He had a small corral and barn for his horses plus an oversize garage where he kept his private vehicle as well as his official county patrol car. There was a light showing under the garage door.

Rory went inside. His brother had his head stuck

under the hood of the black-and-white Chevy Blazer with the police cruiser light bar on top.

"How come you don't have Ernie at the garage fix your truck?"

Eric raised his head too fast and banged it on the raised hood. "Geez, scare a guy, why don't you?" He rubbed the back of his head with his hand.

"Sorry."

"Ernie charges the county too much. I'd rather change my own oil and save the budget for new tires." Picking up a greasy rag, he wiped his hands, all the while studying Rory. "What's wrong?"

He shrugged, playing nonchalant, but felt the gesture came off stiff. "Kristi and my son are leaving tomorrow."

"And?"

"And nothing. She's got to get back to her job, that's all."

Eric leaned back against the fender of the souped up Blazer, still idly wiping his hands. "Do you want her to stay?"

"That's not for me to say." He wandered over to a workbench, fussed with a coil of copper wire and put it down again. "She's got a good job in Spokane."

"Did you *ask* her to stay?"

"Nope. She can make up her own mind."

"And just how is she supposed to do that if she doesn't have all the facts, huh? Tell me that."

"I don't know what facts you're talking about."

"Do you love her, bro?"

Rory tried to look everywhere but at his brother.

Love was a hard thing to admit to anyone, particularly when the person you loved was about to drive out of your life.

"Yeah, I do." The words felt like razor blades in his throat. He'd been afraid to admit his love even to himself. Telling his brother wouldn't help any.

Eric tossed the greasy rag aside. "Bird Brain, I think your dyslexia is making you really stupid. If you love a woman, you've got to tell her."

"What if she doesn't love me back?"

"She had your kid, didn't she?"

"But that only means—"

"Haven't you noticed how Kristi looks at you. Talk about wearing her heart on her sleeve. Tell her how you feel."

"I don't think I can." If Kristi rejected him, it would mean he was no more worthy of love now than when his mother dumped him off at a gas station and drove away with her boyfriend.

"Listen to me, bro. How much worse off would you be if you told her and she told you to get lost?"

"It'd be pretty bad."

"No, it wouldn't," Eric reasoned. "Nothing would change except now you know you've got a son. I'd say that would be on the plus side."

The way Eric put it, it all sounded so reasonable. But it wasn't Eric who would have to put his neck in the noose. Rory would. "How can I ask her to give up her job and move to a town like Grass Valley? She's lived in a city all of her life. Hell, we don't even have a movie theater here. What would she do with her time?"

"I don't know, but Lizzie seems to be doing all right living on the ranch, and she's sure a city girl if I ever saw one. Or she used to be." He rested his hand on Rory's shoulder, gave him a reassuring squeeze. "I know if it were me, I'd give it a shot. You don't have too much to lose."

Rory wasn't that confident. If he was going to tell Kristi he loved her, ask her to marry him, he had to give her a choice that she could live with.

Having failed her once, her happiness was more important than where they lived or a veterinary practice that was just getting off the ground.

But did he have the guts to make the offer he had in mind?

Chapter Fourteen

"How will the wolf find his way back home?"
Perched on the edge of the car seat behind Rory,
Adam plied his father with his usual barrage of questions.

Once again, Rory patiently responded. "Wolves
have a good sense of direction and an uncanny sense
of smell."

In the back of the SUV, the caged wolf eyed his
captors with ill-concealed disdain, his ears laid flat
on his head.

"What if he gets lost?" Adam persisted.

"Wolves are social animals. He'll probably keep
going until he finds a pack to run with."

"Or until he finds his mate," Kristi added.

Rory slanted her a look, his expression softening.
"Yeah, wolves are very loyal to their mates."

Kristi couldn't hold his gaze. Despite her best efforts to do otherwise, in her heart she'd been loyal
to Rory all these years. A bad habit that gained her
little, one that she still couldn't break.

The route to the Durfee cabin looked entirely dif-

ferent than their first trip on snowmobiles. There
were a few muddy spots in the dirt road but no snow
weighing down tree branches and only patches of
dirty white covering the ground in shady areas. The
rest of the snow had melted under the onslaught of
a week's worth of sunny weather.

Just as her hopes and dreams had vanished, leaving
a dreadful ache in her chest.

"What if he wants to stay in the cage?" Adam
asked.

Rory maneuvered the SUV around a young pine
tree that had fallen across the road. "I think he'll be
smarter than that."

"Sometimes people get used to where they are and
can't seem to move on with their lives," Kristi commented, thinking of herself.

"Wolves are a lot smarter than humans that way.
With people it can take a crisis to get them to see
the smart thing to do."

A subtle change in Rory's tone brought Kristi's
head around to look at him. Had it been a new re-
solve she heard? Or was she imagining things?

They rounded the last bend in the road, and the
cabin appeared in a small clearing. Without a mile
high icing of snow, the cabin and field looked less
magical, more grounded in reality than when she had
first seen it. Even so, Kristi could recall every moment she'd spent there with Rory. The way they'd
played in the snow. How he'd kissed her, their
breaths mingling and warming her. Hands palming
his bare chest. His caresses arousing her.

Trembling on the inside, she tried to press away

the memory of him loving her. Tried to lock the love she felt for him back in that old musty box she kept near her heart, never to be opened again.

Rory drew the truck to a stop in the clearing. With Everett Durfee still in Great Falls recovering from his heart attack, no smoke drifted up from the chimney. They had the woods to themselves.

Adam bounded out of the truck. "This is neat! Can we come stay here sometime? Can we? I could bring Troy."

"I don't think so, honey." Kristi exited the vehicle more slowly. "The cabin doesn't belong to us." Only the memories did, and she didn't dare revisit them often.

Rory took his time, examining the clearing and ground around the cabin. Releasing the wolf wouldn't be a problem. What he had to say to Kristi, the words he needed, were knotting his stomach. She could as easily tell him to get lost as accept his proposal. At some level, he expected her to turn him down. He hadn't done much to earn her trust or her love.

He smiled as he caught sight of fresh footprints in the mud by the shed.

"Looks like the female wolf is still hanging around somewhere," he called to Kristi and Adam.

The boy came running. Kristi followed with less enthusiasm. Her interest wasn't in wildlife or animals, he reminded himself, but in human patients. She deserved to pursue the career she'd chosen.

"Look." Holding Adam still, he pointed to the

footprints. "The she-wolf's been around here in the past day or two."

"Wow! *Two* wolves. You think we'll get to see her?"

"I don't know, son. They can be pretty shy."

He and Adam hunkered down, and Rory explained how he could identify the prints as belonging to a wolf and why he knew they were recent. The boy soaked up every bit of information. Someday, if he stayed interested, Adam would make a great wildlife biologist or maybe a veterinarian. Rory hoped he'd be around to share the experience with his son.

Standing, he said, "Okay, let's get our wolf back where he belongs."

Kristi fell into step beside him as they walked back to the truck. "It's wonderful the she-wolf waited for her mate."

"Almost two weeks is a long time in a wolf's life." To ask a woman to wait for nearly six years, to still love a man who had foolishly let her go, seemed unimaginable, yet that was exactly what Rory was hoping for.

Opening the back of the truck, he put the ramp he'd constructed in place and carefully slid the cage down to the ground. A low growl of warning rumbled through the wolf's chest, and the animal pulled his lips back, baring his teeth.

"It's okay, fella. You're almost home."

"Kristi, I need your help to carry the cage to the tree line." He slid a long pole through the wire carrier leaving plenty of room on either side so they

could safely grab it. "Adam, I need you to stay back
out of the way. The wolf's in a bad mood."

"Sometimes Mom gets in a bad mood, and I stay
out of her way."

Suppressing a grin, Rory lifted his side of the cage.
Kristi did the same. Together they walked to a sunny
spot behind the shed. On his command, they set the
cage down on the ground. Kristi backed away.

Slipping the pole free, Rory used it to lift the sliding door open. There was a moment's hesitation as
though he couldn't quite believe his good fortune,
then the wolf burst out of the cage. He raced away
at full gallop with only the slightest hint of a limp.
About thirty feet away he reached a small rise. Turning, he glared back at his captors. Then he tipped his
head back, gave three sharp yips and howled a long,
forsaken sound that rippled through the trees.

A second later a response came, just as lonely and
not too far away.

Rory saw Kristi smile, and he went to her, wrapping his arm around her shoulder.

"She waited for him," he whispered.

"Some females just can't help themselves."

He licked his lips and swallowed hard. "I've been
thinking, Kristi—"

"Look, Mom! Dad! There's two of 'em." The boy
came running up, pointing into the trees, practically
bursting with excitement at the sight of the second,
lighter-colored wolf. "Wait till I tell Troy!"

"Careful, son," Rory warned. "Don't go too
close." Not that the wolves would notice. The pair
was frolicking beneath the trees, rolling around on

the ground, first the female in a submissive position and then, surprisingly, the male taking that role. She nipped at his neck and he returned the favor, little love kisses before they performed another somersault.

"Aren't they beautiful together?" Kristi whispered.

"Looks like that's how they were meant to be." He caught her chin with his fingertips, lifting her face toward him. "I think you and I were meant to be that way, too. Together."

Her eyes widened.

He hurried on before she could say anything. "I know you like your job at the clinic, and I wouldn't want you to have to give it up. You've already sacrificed too much for me, having my baby on your own, raising Adam without me. So I've been thinking I could walk away from my practice, let the bank foreclose, and get a job with another vet in Spokane."

A delicate frown furrowed her forehead. "But a few days ago you thought you had a chance to handle some of the vet cases in Hill County. Why would you want to move to Spokane?"

"Because being here isn't important to me anymore."

She hesitated. Her heart was drumming so hard against her rib cage, she wasn't sure she'd be able to speak over the racket. Desperately, she wanted to be sure what Rory was saying. No more fantasies. This time she wanted the whole truth.

"If you're doing this for Adam, I'm sure we'll be able to work out visitation—"

"It's not just Adam I'm thinking about." He glanced toward their son, who was still safely watching the wolves playfully getting reacquainted. "It's you and me. I love you, Kristi, and I want us to be married. Be a family. I know I messed up before, but if you'll give me a second chance, I'll be the best husband and father I can be. I swear it." Fear and anxiety were written in the strong lines of his face, the dark intensity of his eyes.

The band that had held Kristi's life, her love, in check for almost six years snapped, freeing her heart to soar. The relief was almost painful, the sensation was so all encompassing, and she couldn't catch her breath.

"I'll understand if you don't want to marry me—"

"No." She blurted out the word.

His face fell. The hurt was almost too much for her.

"I mean no, you shouldn't move to Spokane or give up your practice here. I've got a better idea."

He blinked and shook his head. "What idea?"

"Grandma Justine wants to retire or at least cut back on her hours. She's thinking of selling her practice to a doctor in Great Falls."

"And?" he prompted, confused by her apparent switch in topic.

"I don't necessarily think it would be the best thing for Grandma to retire, not entirely, at least. But whether she sells her practice or stays, a nurse practitioner could run most of the operation under the guidance of an M.D.''

"You're saying you would consider living in Grass Valley?"

He looked so thoroughly puzzled, she took pity on the man. Palming his cheek, she said, "Rory, I've never stopped loving you. Not from the moment I met you. I'll live in Grass Valley for the rest of my life, but only under one condition."

A relieved smile teased around the corners of his mouth. "Name your condition, and if it's within my power, it's yours."

"All I've ever wanted is to be your wife and have your children. Think you could manage that?"

He didn't speak. Instead, he pulled her into his arms, his deep, drugging kiss all the answer she needed.

The spring sun warmed them from above as they held each other, finally coming together after a long absence. But it was Rory's love that warmed Kristi's heart. She knew, this time, she'd never be alone again.

"I love you," she whispered against his lips.

"I love you, too, Sparkles." He smiled, and a low chuckle rumbled in his chest. "I've gotta be the luckiest man in the world."

"Hey!" Adam complained. "What are you guys doing?"

Kristi reached out her hand to her son, and Rory hefted the boy into their embrace. The youngster's legs wrapped around his father's waist.

"Honey, your father and I are going to get married. How does that sound?"

The boy's cheeks glowed with excitement and from all the fresh air. Montana was a healthy place to raise her son.

He glanced at his father. "Does that mean you're gonna move to Spokane with us?"

"Your mom has a better idea. How 'bout you and she move here with me? You could be my official junior veterinarian's assistant."

"I could?"

"You bet. Whenever you want."

Rory brushed a kiss on his son's cheek, bringing a lump to Kristi's throat. They'd be a family now, the three of them, and maybe there would be more babies in the future. Her dream was coming true. Her happiness made her feel as if she was floating on air—until a tiny scowl wrinkled Adam's face.

"Will you come to Spokane at least *once* so I can show Troy I gots a dad?"

"I will. I promise."

"Oh, my gosh. I didn't think. I *have* to go back to Spokane today," Kristi said with a gasp. "I can't leave the clinic in the lurch—"

"It's okay." With his free arm, Rory gave her a hug. "I'll make sure I free up my schedule for next weekend and come for a visit. I wouldn't want Troy to think my son is a liar."

Kristi thought that would satisfy Adam's concern, but he was still frowning. "What's wrong now, honey?"

"Does this mean I'm gonna be Adam William Little Gray Wolf Kerrigan Oakes now?"

Kristi caught Rory's eye and smiled. "I guess so. And I get to be Mrs. Rory Oakes. Pretty neat, huh?"

Adam didn't seem nearly as pleased as she was. "Mom, how am I gonna write that whole big long name on top of my papers at school? I'm gonna be in big trouble with Miss Zidbeck. I'll never get my work done in time."

Unable to help herself, Kristi laughed out loud. So did Rory.

Adam didn't know what was so funny until his father said, "Don't worry about it, champ. We're a family now and we love each other. If any of us gets into trouble, we'll work it out together. I promise."

THE WEDDING TOOK PLACE in the middle of June at the church in Grass Valley. To Rory it looked as though the entire town population plus most of the ranchers who lived within a fifty-mile radius had turned out for the event. Of course, Kristi's mom was there as well as her friends from Spokane.

Rory had never sweated about anything as much as he had this wedding. He'd been scared spitless that Kristi would change her mind. And this morning before the wedding, he'd been afraid he would pass out, he'd been so nervous.

Now, at the potluck reception held in the church recreation hall—which included a half-dozen different potato salads—he was downright cocky. He'd made it through the ceremony without fainting. The honeymoon came next. His confidence soared. He could handle that.

Eric clasped Rory's shoulder, giving it a squeeze. "You did good, Bird Brain. You're a lucky fellow to snare Kristi."

"You won't get any argument out of me, White

Eyes.'' Both Eric and Walker had been his grooms-men; Adam was his best man, and proud as punch to stand up in front of the entire congregation.

''Guess that leaves me to uphold the reputation of the Oakes boys as carefree bachelors,'' Eric said.

Glancing across the room where Kristi was schmoozing with some of the ladies, Rory was grateful he no longer qualified as a bachelor. He knew Eric wasn't the confirmed bachelor he wanted to let on, either. As adolescents, all the brothers had talked about someday having their own families, being fathers to their own kids, blood of their blood. To kids growing up without their birth parents, that was doubly important. They all had needed to reaffirm their rightful place in the world. Eric hadn't found his yet.

''You'll find someone,'' Rory said to him. ''Wait and see.''

''Take a look around, bro. The pickings are somewhere between dismal and zero.''

Rory had to admit every woman in the room was married or underage. That made for a pretty poor selection. ''Guess you'll have to take a fishing trip. They say there are a lot of unattached females in Denver.''

''Thanks, but no. I figure I'm a lot better off if I stay right here where I belong. After my years on the rodeo circuit, I got my fill of women who wanted to latch on to anyone who wore jeans and a Stetson.''

''Who knows. If you stay put, the perfect woman for you may show up at your front door one of these days.''

''Not very likely. Grass Valley isn't exactly on a well-traveled tourist route.''

Rory had a lot better things to do than carry on a lengthy discussion about the merits of marriage with his brother. Namely, he wanted to claim his wife and begin their wedded bliss.

Walking away from Eric, Rory headed toward Kristi. As though she felt him coming, she turned and smiled.

"I think it's time we got out of here, Mrs. Oakes."

Her blue eyes sparkled as brightly as sky rockets on the Fourth of July. "Whatever you say, Dr. Oakes."

Minutes later they kissed Adam goodbye. Knowing he was going to stay at the Double O with a gazillion cousins and the same number of horses, he didn't give his parents' departure a second thought.

That didn't trouble either Rory or Kristi. There'd be plenty of time later to bond their small family together. These next few days belonged to *them,* and Rory intended to make good use of every single minute.

* * * * *

Don't miss Eric's story
next month in Charlotte Maclay's
MONTANA TWINS.
Available only from
Harlequin American Romance!

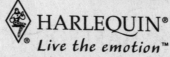

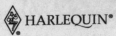

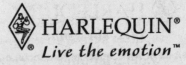

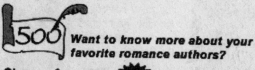

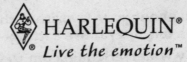

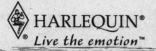

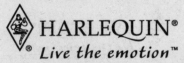